A MUTUALLY BENEFICIAL MISTAKE

The Unexpected Series Book Two

HARPER REED

ISBN: 979-8839920446

Cover Credit—JoY Author Designs

Editor: Jamie Holmes

Dedication

To all the sunshine's of the world...
May you find your grumpier half and enjoy torturing them
for the rest of your days.

Contents

Chapter One

DIRTY LITTLE BITCHES

Kenzie

EATING A BANANA SHOULD *NOT* TURN ME ON. Except, it's been months since I've been on a date with a man worthy of taking home, and my battery-operated boyfriends can only do so much and for so long. So, here I am, at my desk, surrounded by mostly nerdy computer dudes and feeling needy as fuck with no prospects in sight.

"McKenzie?" a soft but sure voice calls from around my cubical wall.

I turn my head, mentally shaking away my inappropriate thoughts, and find my boss's assistant Clara standing there in her blue plaid skirt, matching blazer, and black Mary Jane shoes.

"How can I help you?" I ask, trying to keep the trepidation out of my voice. I don't like it when Joslin wants to see me or needs something from me. She's harder on me than on the rest of my co-workers for reasons she's never outright said, but I have my assumptions.

"Mrs. Croft would like to speak with you," Clara says with a smile, but it doesn't quite reach her eyes, making my nerves worse.

I give her a terse nod. "I'll be there just as soon as this program loads that I'm working on."

Clara bites the inside of her cheek and shakes her head. "Mrs. Croft insisted you come right away."

A heavy sigh exits from between my lips. "Of course."

I glance over at Glen who is nearest to me. "Will you make sure this finishes?" Then, I point to my computer.

He pushes his glasses further up his nose and rubs a hand over his shaved, balding head while looking at my screen. "Is that the new project we just launched last week? Shouldn't you already have access to that?"

Sometimes I wonder how some of these guys still have a job. "No, it's the updates we'll be doing in two weeks. I'm testing them today and need this beta version to download first. Just keep an eye on it and don't touch anything unless the computer starts making noises it shouldn't."

His eyes never leave my screen. "Sure thing, Mac."

I grit my teeth. I hate when they call me that, and every employee within our little cubical city knows it. Kenzie is the only shortened version of my name that I prefer, but I don't bother to remind Glen of that. At least not now when Joslin is waiting on me.

Getting up, I see that the assistant is gone, and I make my way toward the boss's office on my own. I never thought I'd find myself working in tech, but after taking a coding class in college just for fun, I found myself enthralled with the problem-solving aspects. It was like taking a Rubik's cube of letters and numbers and finding a way for them to form something useful.

Yes, I realize that sounds incredibly nerdy and boring, but it's a high for me unlike anything else. Well, other than orgasmic sex.

And there I go again, thinking about getting laid when that's the last thing I need to have going through my brain while at work. There isn't a single soul in Global Tech's building that I would date. I don't need that kind of drama in my life. Especially not when most men can't handle a woman who speaks whatever is on her mind.

I like to blame Ella for my recent rise in standards. My best friend had to go and land herself the perfect man that she just got engaged to a couple weeks ago. Now, more often than not, I find my dates boring or inappropriate in all the worst ways.

I give my head a solid shake when I arrive at Joslin's corner of the fourth floor. Clara quickly smiles at me before going back to shuffling papers on her desk.

My knuckles rap on the door and it pops open. "Mrs. Croft?"

"Come in, McKenzie." Her tone is flat, and when I enter, she's typing furiously on her computer with a glower on her oval face.

Her blonde hair is twisted up into a perfect bun, and she's wearing a sleek gray pantsuit with a crisp white blouse beneath the jacket. Her back is ramrod straight as she types without looking at the keyboard, and I'm in awe with how in control she seems even when she looks pissed.

Oh, shit. Did I screw something up? Did I forget to update a program for one of her projects? If I'm about to get fired, I'm going to... I don't know, but something, because I've been working my ass off these last few months for Global Tech.

"Sit, McKenzie," she says while still typing and without looking at me.

I do as she commands, keeping my ankles crossed as I tug at my green sweater, then wipe my palms over my whitewash jeans. I don't dress up for work. I don't "people" much around here, and there isn't a fancy dress code for my position, so I don't see the point, but I'm suddenly feeling out of place and underdressed sitting at Joslin's desk.

Another minute passes as I switch between twisting my fingers together and crossing and uncrossing my ankles.

Joslin finally gives me her full attention, her honey eyes peering at me while her thin lips create a flat line. She makes an odd humming noise and then slides a piece of paper across the glass desktop toward me.

Her finger taps on the list of projects that are typed out. "You've worked on all of these, yes?"

I nod, staying quiet because it seems like the safe thing to do until I know why she's called me in here.

"And while you haven't been the lead on all of them, you've overseen their executions, repairs, and updates, right?"

Oh, God. Am I going to get in trouble for doing my job *too* well? Fuck my life.

"Yes, but I didn't mean to overstep. I always asked the lead before I did anything," I say a little too quickly.

Joslin finally grins. "I know, McKenzie. You're not in trouble, so don't have a heart attack. That's paperwork I don't have time to fill out."

I wait for her to laugh at the joke, but the sound never comes.

"So, why am I here?" I finally ask, leaning a little closer to the desk.

Joslin folds her hands in front of her and frowns. "Global Tech is doing some restructuring." She pauses when her computer dings.

She takes her sweet time reading whatever just popped up on her screen, and I'm nearly dying in my seat while I wait for her to finish that damn sentence.

Her eyes land on me again. "My apologies. It hasn't been a great day for everyone around here, but hopefully, it's about to be for you."

My face scrunches. "What do you mean?"

Joslin leans back in her chair, relaxing for the first time since I walked into her office.

"I've been charged with cutting the dead weight around here and finding proper replacements. As much as it pains me to do this, because I don't want to lose you from the ground level—"

She cuts off again, and her attention is back on her computer.

I want to grab this woman by her suit coat and shake her. She said I wasn't in trouble, but it sure as hell sounds like I'm getting canned.

If that happens...Global Tech is about to see a whole different side of McKenzie Chase.

She begins to mutter. "Stupid, stubborn men. I swear, sometimes I hate my job." Then, she looks at me again and forces a smile to her face. "Again, I apologize for the interruptions."

Damn, Joslin is being too...considerate? Professional? I don't know what, but it's damn sure not her normal. I'm totally getting fired for some stupid bullshit.

"As I was saying, I'm not looking forward to replacing you, but when Frank came to me with this proposal, I knew you were the right person for the job."

I raise a brow and let out a breath. "So, you're not letting me go, but I do have to transfer departments?"

I wasn't sure this was better.

Joslin pulls another paper from her desk and hands it to me. "Yes and no. You're getting a promotion, and while you won't work in the weeds of coding any longer, you'll still be working under me, right here on the fourth floor."

As I accept the paper, I try to focus on the words while she keeps talking.

"The work you've been doing this year hasn't gone unnoticed, McKenzie. Not by me or any of the other managers in our department. You're a lot like I was when I was in your position, and I've only pushed you so hard because I can see what you're capable of. Look this over and tell me what you think."

I hold the sheet between my fingers and scan the contents. A promotion is the last thing I expected or have even thought about, especially one that has me supervising other employees. This one also comes with a pay raise and plenty of other bullet points lined out. Mentions of my own office—no more cubical city—quarterly bonuses, and project management duties capture my eye, and... What's that?

"What does 'volunteer hours' mean exactly?" I ask, looking up at Joslin.

She peeks at the paper where I'm pointing. "Oh, that. All employees in supervisor positions are encouraged to volunteer somewhere locally at least twenty hours a year. You can use work hours to get them done as long as you're not behind on any projects."

Volunteer? More like volun-*told*.

"If you're unsure where to spend your time, I probably have something for you," she adds when I merely continue to stare at the sheet, not missing the number of zeroes in my new salary.

I wasn't prepared for this kind of offer, but the more I read over the information, the more I'm smiling and nodding.

This could change everything. I've always wanted to work hard for my money and livelihood, and while I've been content with my simple lifestyle, there are certain things I'd love to do. Like buy a house, or go on vacation without having to put half of the trip on a credit card, or buy that stupidly expensive purse I don't actually need, but really want.

"I'll do it," I say.

She grins. "Good. I already told them you'd start as soon as the announcement is made."

I laugh, but before I can say anything, Joslin continues, "I'll email you the information for the volunteer position I think you'd be a good fit for later today or tomorrow. I just need to double check a few things. It may be temporary, but it will fill your quota for this year."

My mouth pops open. "I still have to get twenty hours by the end of the year even though it's already August?"

"If you want a good annual review, then you do." Her

computer dings again, and instead of keeping her from other work, I offer my sincere thanks and stand.

She nods and mutters more to herself while I see myself out.

I'm grinning from ear to ear when I exit, and Clara smiles at me, handing me more papers. "Congratulations, McKenzie. Sorry I was quiet before. I didn't want to give anything away."

I chuckle. "I thought I was getting fired, so you did a great job hiding the truth."

She gestures to the papers. "Those are the rest of the information you'll need about your new role in Project Management. Please email me if you have any questions."

"Will do."

There's a skip in my step as I make my way back to my computer, and my mood rises when I find that the program I needed downloaded just as I wanted.

Glen tries to talk to me, but I put my earbuds in. Nobody can ruin this day. I'm going to get my work done, review the papers Clara gave me, and then celebrate with my two best friends Ella and Piper tonight.

———

THOSE DIRTY LITTLE BITCHES. THEY STOOD ME UP. I'm sitting at our favorite bar with a margarita pitcher in front of me and three glasses, yet there is only one of me.

Ella's earlier headache turned into a full-blown migraine that has her sleeping next to the toilet, and Piper had to work late. Sure, she just got a promotion herself, so I can understand, but I don't want to.

I want to laugh and scream and be excited with my girls. Instead, I fill all three glasses on the tabletop and intend to drink each of them myself.

I can at least get drunk before I call for a ride back home. To my studio apartment. With nobody in it. All by myself.

Fuck. I'm supposed to be happy right now. Not moping.

My eyes scan the bar, and I look for anyone else by themselves. Maybe I can invite them to join me. Potential one-night stand or friendly face, it doesn't make a difference. I just don't want to be alone.

The room is surrounded by dark wood beams and cream walls with pipe accents followed by twinkle style lights strung all around, making it rather dim in the bar. A perfect setting when you're drinking and want some privacy, but not so great when you're looking for a new companion.

I sit a little straighter when I spot a young woman carrying a single drink away from the bar. She scans the crowd, passing over me, and her eyes land on the group three tables over. Damn it.

Then, I spot a sexy man in a suit coming in the door. His eyes are icy blue and the first thing I notice. The next is the scowl creasing his face and taking away from his straight jawline and five o'clock shadow.

He adjusts his forest-green tie and glances around. Our eyes never connect, but I watch him intently. The suit is a perfect fit. Not a seam out of place or a sleeve too short on his well-over-six-foot frame.

My tongue darts out to wet my lips, and I take a long

pull of my margarita. Damn. Normally, I'm not attracted to rich, stuffy men and he seems to fit that bill pretty accurately as he takes a seat at the bar—alone—but for him? And tonight? I'm willing to make an exception.

I finish my drink and move to slide out of my metal bar stool, but he pulls a phone from his inner front pocket and starts talking.

Sigh. Maybe I can steal his attention later.

I'm halfway through my second drink and nearly ready to give up on the night when an elderly woman walks into the bar, gasping loudly when the bell over the door rings. Her hand presses against her chest and she glances up at the ceiling before continuing forward.

I chuckle, and our stares meet. I assume she's here to meet someone, but instead, she comes right over to me.

"Where are your friends?" She points a wrinkly finger to the other two glasses.

"At home, being party poopers," I say with a sigh.

Her hands pull up on her light-pink pants. "They should try Depends. Might help them get out more."

She takes a seat, and I offer her the remaining full glass. I watch her sniff the sugared edge, shrug, then take a drink. A small bit dribbles down her lip and lands on her flower print shirt.

"Shit. I just bought this."

I nearly choke at her choice in words. "Put a little rubbing alcohol on it when you're home and it will be just fine after washing."

She looks me up and down with a smirk on her wrinkly face. "Spill a few drinks in your nights?"

I shrug. "Possibly."

"I'm Louise." She extends her hand, and I accept the gesture.

"Kenzie," I say, then finish my second drink and reach for the pitcher to fill it back up.

I didn't intend to party it up with Grandma, but the lonely can't be choosy. I'll take her. Though, my eyes cut to the businessman at the bar again. He would have been an excellent candidate as well.

Louise must follow my stare, because she says, "If you take a picture, you can think of him when you're home later taking care of business."

Once again, I can't breathe, and I end up snorting so loud that half the bar turns our way. Including the hottie from the bar.

He cuts a glare at me while he continues to speak into the phone. Okay, maybe he wouldn't have been a great choice in...whatever my dirty mind was conjuring.

My attention swivels back to Louise. "What brings you out tonight?"

She hiccups, her drink almost half gone already. "This place used to be a speakeasy when I was your age. It's where I met my husband. Today should be our fifty-fifth anniversary, but my Marty passed away last year. I thought revisiting where we met might cheer me up."

My mood turns, and my heart aches for her. I move to reach for her hand on the table and offer my condolences, but she pulls it away.

"I lived most of my life with the most wonderful man in the world and made decades of memories with him and our family. I don't need anyone to be sad for me. If anything, you should be jealous." She smiles and continues sipping her stolen drink.

I laugh, this time quieter. "You know, a few months ago, I would have told you I wasn't in the slightest, but now? Yeah, I think I am."

She nods toward the businessman. "Why don't you go make another new friend and take care of your problem, then?"

I shake my head. "Things aren't as simple as they used to be."

She raises a gray brow at me. "Aren't they, though? You find the person you're attracted to, chat with them, make sure they're not a murderer, and then voila!"

Louise flicks her fingers like she's making fireworks with her hands, and I chuckle again. "You make it sound so easy."

"And your generation makes everything so complicated."

I raise my glass toward her. "Amen, Louise."

We sit in companionable silence while we both enjoy our margaritas and the classic rock playing from the speakers around the bar.

When Louise finishes first, she sighs and leans forward. "Well, Kenzie, it was lovely to meet you, but I've done what I came here to do. Maybe I'll see you around."

I'm mid-sip when she slips off her stool, and by the time I can use my voice again, she's already halfway to the door.

Loneliness creeps back in, and I find myself looking toward my right for the umpteenth time. Though, I swear to myself that it's not to peek at the hottie's broad shoulders or to notice how the ends of his finger-length russet hair curl just over the collar of his shirt.

Nope. Absolutely not.

Before I do something I probably shouldn't, I head to the bathroom—taking my newly refilled drink with me, because a girl can never be too careful—and a part of me hopes he's gone by the time I return.

Chapter Two

EAT A DICK

Bentley

I THOUGHT I KNEW HOW BAD JET LAG COULD BE, but somehow, I've surpassed the tiredness of my flight from Cusco, Peru to home in Charlotte, North Carolina and entered a state of delirium I've never experienced before.

I try to count the hours it's been since I've properly slept, but all I know is it's nearing two full days. I should have taken some sleeping pills when I got home, but the idea of showing up at my new job sounded better.

That was until I pulled into the parking lot of West-to-East, Inc. and realized what a dick I would look like, dropping in unannounced for my first official visit right as everyone was supposed to be heading home for the day.

So, I left just as quickly as I arrived, but instead of going back home like I should have, I found myself at a local bar I've never been to and hoping for an evening by myself to unwind from my trip. Only, my phone keeps ringing, preventing me from enjoying my hop-heavy beer.

First, it was my sister, making sure I'd made it home and berating me for not checking in with her once I was back at my house.

Now, it's Selene.

I know I shouldn't answer. I know better after our last break-up, but I can't stop my thumb from pressing that green button as her name lights up on my screen. A bad decision that I blame on the jet lag.

"Hello, Bentley," she coos, and the pitch of her voice is like nails on a chalkboard for me. Another reminder of why I shouldn't have taken the call.

"What do you want, Selene?" I ask with a heavy sigh and feel the creases on my face deepening.

She scoffs with shock. "I miss you, and as soon as Celia told me you were due back today, I couldn't wait any longer to hear your voice."

My fucking sister. Clearly, I need to remind her that *my* business is my own. Not information that needs to be shared with my *ex*-girlfriends.

"Well, I'm busy, so we'll have to chat later," I say and pull the phone away to hang up, but her tone lowers and she calls my name.

"I just... I don't like the way we ended things before you left," she says.

My chuckle turns dark quickly. "You mean you'd like to apologize for saying that my volunteering to help better the communities in third-world countries was a waste of my time since it didn't further my standing within our circles?"

She makes a noise that sounds like she's trying to force herself to cry.

"I *am* sorry, Benny. I didn't mean any of what I said. I

just want you back. We belong together. I feel that in my soul."

The way she calls me "Benny" makes me want to stab myself in the eye. The rest of what she has to say used to work on me every time we broke up, but not anymore. I've seen her true colors a few too many times and I won't go back to that life. Not ever again.

"Nothing has changed, Selene. We broke up for the final time, and we're not getting back together just because I'm home and you've apologized."

She huffs, and all sounds of sadness are gone from her tone. "We're not over, Bentley. I won't accept that."

Then, she hangs up. On me. That woman really is a piece of work.

When my sister introduced us, I thought Selene was a nice person. She played her part almost too well, always talking about how much she loved her family, and how work was something that gave her a purpose, and about the kids she wanted to have because growing up an only child had been torturous for her.

Then, as the months passed and I got to see other sides of her, I realized she is just like my mother. Selene is only looking for a retirement plan in a husband. She wants to be pampered and taken care of. She has no interest in making a difference in the world with our resources.

That woman is everything I never wanted to be after the way I grew up.

Outsiders always look at the rich and think they have it so easy, but growing up with parents who only cared about their bank accounts wasn't anything I wish to repeat for my own life.

For a short time, I thought Selene felt the same way I did about the way we grew up, but after breaking up and getting back together a couple of times, I've finally realized what we were doing was the definition of insanity. We want very different things out of life, and nothing is ever going to work between us, no matter how much time apart we have.

Fuck. My mood has soured, and I have to piss. I toss a hundred to the bartender who gasps, then I walk off.

I take care of business in the bathroom and exit just in time for the redhead I'd seen earlier to run right into me. Cool, sticky liquid splashes over the front of my new suit, and I step back, pulling the ruined fabric away from my skin.

Her hazel eyes roam over my now see-through dress shirt and she hums. "Well, hello."

"Watch where you're going," I snap.

The flush on her fair cheeks darkens. "Excuse me? You ran into me."

I bark out a deep laugh. "Right, because you were headed toward the men's bathroom to do what exactly?"

It's the only door left down this hallway. She's too drunk to even know which way she was supposed to be going.

"No, I was...looking for a quiet corner...to make a call," she says, her voice lacking the confidence to convince me her words are the truth.

"Right. Well, thanks for ruining my suit." Then, I rake my eyes over her simple green sweater, light jeans with holes in them that are supposed to be fashionable, and back up to her face before shaking my head.

The action isn't necessary, but I'm already annoyed, and she only made things worse by running into me.

I try to brush past her, but she grabs on to my arm, then gestures up and down my body with her other hand. There's fire in her hazel eyes, and her jaw tightens while she stares daggers in my direction.

"Just because you're a rich prick, that doesn't give you the right to look down on me."

I move forward, stepping closer until our faces are only inches apart. "You don't know anything about me."

Her chest expands, and she squares her soft shoulders. "Your five-thousand-dollar suit tells me enough."

"Try *ten* thousand," I goad for no good reason.

Damn, she smells like strawberries and honey.

She shoves me back, sobering by the seconds that I continue to piss her off. "Go back to Madison Park and eat a dick." She turns, then mutters, "And to think I wanted to take him home."

I know she's talking to herself, but I don't miss the disappointment in her quiet tone.

I reach for her wrist and spin her back around. I don't know what I'm doing. I shouldn't touch her. I should let her walk away, but fuck, I suddenly don't want to. Another thing I can blame on the jet lag. Later.

She sucks in a breath, and I pin her against the wall. "How about *I* take *you* home?"

Instead of answering me, she grabs the sides of my face roughly and jerks my head down. Her tongue demands entry into my mouth, and my already-hardening dick stiffens to full mast while she searches every corner of my mouth.

I press my hips against her, and the moan that slips from her mouth is fuel to the sudden inferno inside my body.

My hands tangle with hers, and I drag her from the dark hallway. Unless she has any objections to getting in my car, then I'm about to fuck the snark right out of this fiery woman.

Chapter Three

A GOOD FUCKING

Kenzie

THOUGHTS OF WHICH BATTERY-OPERATED boyfriend I am going to use tonight enter my mind the moment I turn my back on that douche of a rich prick, but that's before he reaches for me.

I don't expect his touch to burn like it is, and I sure as hell don't expect his mouth to make my thong wet. Yet, both things are happening.

I don't even know his name, but as he guides me toward the exit, I can't make myself care one damn bit.

I *need* this. I need a release of the sexual kind, and what better way to celebrate my promotion than with a delicious one-night stand.

Sure, he could be horrible in bed, but the way he dominated my mouth in that hallway tells me that I probably don't need to worry about that.

He leads us outside. When we get to the corner of the

21

brick building, he pushes me against the rough wall, his hands barely touching me this time.

"First, I don't live in Madison Park. I live in Providence," he says, and my chuckle cuts him off.

"Same thing."

He narrows his azure eyes on me and continues, "Second, are you sure you want to get in my car?"

He searches my face, and the fact that he's making sure I'm coherent enough to be making a sound decision, such as fucking a complete stranger, has me wanting to jump him right here in public.

I sneak my hand between us and grip his hard, impressive length. "Abso-fucking-lutely."

A hiss escapes through his clenched teeth, and he wraps an arm around my waist, practically carrying me through the parking lot while he fishes his keys out of his pocket with his free hand.

I'm tempted to offend more of his rich-ness when I see the lights blinking on a blacked-out Range Rover, but I decide better of it.

If I screw the pooch on this, I'll kick my own ass.

Mostly because I need a good fucking like I need my next breath.

Still, I'm not an idiot. I take note of his license plate number. I'll text the info to Piper and Ella just as soon as I have a second without him watching me.

He opens my door and lifts me into the SUV. While I settle into the plush leather seat and start to buckle, I realize he's still standing there, staring at me.

I raise a brow at him. "Something on my face?"

He glowers and braces himself against the doorframe. "You don't even know my name."

"And you don't know mine."

His fingers curl tighter around the metal. "This is a poor choice on your part."

I pull my phone from my back pocket and wiggle it at him. "I already memorized your license plate number. As soon as you shut the door, I'll be texting that information along with Providence to my friends. They'll send the cavalry if they don't wake up to a text from me saying I'm okay."

He grunts, stares some more, then finally says, "I'm Bentley."

"Kenzie." I grin. "Are we good now or should I call an uber and plan on taking care of what you started on my own once I'm home?"

Instead of answering, he glances at my thighs where my fingers are spread, then slams the door closed. I watch him stiffly make his way around the front of the vehicle, then I text Ella and Piper just as planned.

Me: Since you bitches didn't come celebrate with me, I'm going home with someone. Providence area. Range Rover. FML-6874.

Piper: Be safe. Make him wear a condom. Even if he sounds rich.

Ella: Have fun and let us know when you're home!
Me: Of course.

I love those two more than my own life.

Bentley is already pulling out of the parking spot by the time I'm done, and I wave my phone at him again.

"Safety precautions taken. Does that make you feel better?" I taunt.

"Not having my suit soaked in tequila would make me *feel* better," he gripes.

I laugh. "I'm sure you have a dozen more hanging in your big walk-in closet."

His icy eyes turn dark, and he mutters something under his breath that I don't catch. Though, that doesn't deter me. To keep the mood from plummeting away, I reach over to start helping him with his problem.

My fingers deftly work at the forest-green tie around his neck. I don't miss the way the muscles in his neck strain or how his hands tighten around the steering wheel.

"What are you doing?" he asks with a small grumble in his voice.

I yank the tie loose. "Helping."

I pop a few of the buttons to his white dress shirt open, and he grabs my hand. "Not *helping*, Kenzie."

Shit. The way his voice deepens while he says my name makes me press my thighs closer together. I've never been one to be attracted to grumpy, rich dudes, but maybe I've been missing out.

I move back to my seat, grinning the whole way to his house. It's been a long time since I've done anything like this. Probably not since I was twenty-one. Ugh. That was almost a decade ago. Not something I need to think about right now.

Bentley slows his Range Rover down when we enter the Providence community. I keep my phone in my hands and plan to text the exact address to my friends once I can see the house.

I've never had any reason to roam through this neighborhood. The mansion-sized houses, gated entries, and eight-foot-tall privacy fences remind me why.

I might not have grown up poor, but this was never the lifestyle I wanted.

Though, it would be for tonight.

Bentley pulls into a driveway, one with no privacy fence and no fancy automated gate. It's one of the few properties that remain open like that in this whole area.

Interesting.

The house is massive just like the rest, though. It's at least two stories—maybe three if he has a lower level that can't be seen from the street. The exterior is covered in brick, and the windows all have white shutters around them that match the columns holding up the covered porch at the double mahogany main doors.

The half-circle driveway curves around, but Bentley goes straight ahead and pulls into the four-car garage. When he shuts the vehicle down, I send my friends the address before tucking my phone away. Hopefully I won't need it again until I've been thoroughly ravished.

I open my own door and meet Bentley at the front of his car. I glance around, and I'm surprised to find an old Harley motorcycle in mid-restoration at the other end of the garage.

I nod that way. "Are you doing that yourself?"

"Did you come here to ask questions?" he counters.

I purse my lips. "I guess not."

He leads the way into his house, and I'm greeted with walnut hardwood floors and a kitchen any cook would die for. There are two ovens, eight burners on the stove, stainless steel appliances, and sleek black countertops between the light-gray cabinets.

Bentley has already moved ahead while I gawked, so I lengthen my stride to catch up. We come out of the kitchen and into a formal dining room that doesn't look used. It seems more like a prop in a house too big for one man.

Through the next archway, I see the front doors ahead, and on my right is a large wooden staircase. Bentley is already on the third step when he glances back at me. "Coming?"

I smirk and flick my hair back. "I hope to be soon."

I expect a returning grin, but he merely continues up the steps.

"Listen, if you don't want me here any longer, I'll leave," I say before following him further.

He might be hot, and I'm definitely needy, but I don't want a pity fuck.

Bentley comes back down the stairs with heavy footsteps, removing the tie I'd already undone as he does, and then drops it to the ground. He stalks toward me, then grips my waist with both hands when he reaches me. "If I didn't want you here, then you wouldn't be. Now, let's go upstairs, so I can fuck that smirk off your face."

Holy. Shit.

I'm trembling and wet when he picks me up and throws me over his shoulder. I squeal for a second, but I don't fight him. He goes left once we're on the second level, and we enter a set of cream-colored doors. I expect him to set me down once we're in his room, but before I can even look around, he turns sharply and walks into the bathroom.

It's nearly as big as the bedroom I didn't really get to see and has a shower with four shower heads. One on each of the three tiled walls and another, bigger head hanging down from the ceiling.

"I need to wash your drink off me and you're going to help," he says with authority.

I'm very tempted to be defiant, but again, I quell the need and start stripping my clothes off.

By the time I'm naked, Bentley hasn't even finished unbuttoning his shirt. I decide to poke the bear in a more positive way.

I walk into the shower and my feet step onto gloriously warm tiles. I wiggle my toes as I turn the shower on. All four heads spout water, and I manage to hold in my yelp while I wait for the water to quickly warm around me.

The door and front enclosure of the shower are glass, so I know Bentley can see everything I'm doing without having to look his way. I use that to my advantage and turn sideways before leaning my head under the ceiling showerhead and trailing my hands slowly down the front of me.

My left hand stops at my breast and gives my nipple a little squeeze while letting the right hand continue its downward motion. My fingers slip over my bare folds and put pressure just where I know I like.

I tilt my head back under the spray of water, and soft moans build inside me as I add another finger to the mix. I'm more than eager to get off, especially when I know Bentley is watching me. I curl a finger inside me and arch forward, still keeping my eyes closed.

A cool breeze enters the shower, and I fight a smile.

He broke first.

Bentley's big hands reach for me. One lifts my head and the other removes my hand from my pussy. "Do you have any shame?"

I finally meet his heady stare. "Nope. Not when it comes to knowing what I want and not being afraid to take it."

His palm cups my center, and one finger dips inside me but pauses. "There's not going to be a need for self-pleasuring tonight."

My thighs press together, and I'm ready for him to fuck me senseless already.

I cast my eyes down to find his dick standing at attention and several inches bigger than I expected. I kind of thought he might have been compensating for something with his suit and fancy car, but it's clearly not for his body parts.

My fingers wrap around his cock, and I squeeze. "Then, *you* better start pleasuring me."

His chest rumbles before he picks me up and sits down on the tile bench underneath the right showerhead. The spray goes out far enough that the water won't be drowning us while I ride the fuck out of him.

My knees settle on each side of him, and my chest is right in his face. His mouth moves forward and captures a nipple before sucking hard on the pebbled skin.

I tilt my head back and move my hand between us to guide myself on top of him.

"Fuck. Condom," I tell him.

Bentley pulls back just far enough to say, "Right knee."

I lean forward and spot the foil on the bench. Oh, this

beautiful, prepared man. He must have tossed it there when my eyes were still closed.

I don't hesitate to grab it and unroll the rubber over his dick while he starts devouring my neck, thanks to my forward position.

As soon as I'm done, he grabs my hips, and I hold the base of his cock just long enough to position the wide head against my pussy.

When I'm out of the way, Bentley jerks his hips up and I press down at the same time. I let out a loud gasp when I have to stretch more than I'm prepared for to accommodate him.

Fuck. He's not even all the way in, and I'm already full.

"Again," he demands.

My body shudders and I relax, taking the rest of him on his second thrust. I rock forward against his pelvic bone, and goosebumps rise up on my arms.

His hand moves up my spine, and he yanks on the long strands of my auburn hair until my face is nearly in the water.

Just when I'm sure he's going to drown me, his other arm curls around my waist, holding me in place while he pounds into me.

Light sprays of water sprinkle onto my face, but I couldn't give two fucks. Not any longer.

My hands grip his thighs underneath me, holding on to them for leverage, because it's the only thing I can do while this man owns the fuck out of my pussy.

"I'm going to come," I warn when I start to see stars in my eyes.

Bentley merely grunts in reply and tightens his hold on me while increasing his speed.

My nails dig into his skin, and my back curves inward. I drop my head back further, my forehead finally getting drenched by the water spray. Except, with the contractions building inside me and the heat unfurling at my core, I hardly notice.

Holy fuck. What is this man doing to me? Everything inside me feels like it's on fire.

Bentley's palm draws me forward until I'm sitting up again instead of leaning away from him, and the change in position combined with his relentless thrusts has me crying out and gripping tightly to his shoulders.

I ride out the tsunami, trying to get my wits back. Every time I open my eyes, I'm still seeing stars.

Bentley's arms encase me, and he stands, keeping my body low enough that his throbbing cock is still buried inside me. His steps put us under the spray of the water.

"Wash my chest off," he demands.

I glance up at him, his words bringing me back to reality. "Excuse me?"

He nods to the soap dispensers. "Clean up your mess."

Oh, Mr. Businessman is a dominant. Unfortunately for him, so am I.

"Say please."

His eyes darken, and his sculpted lips thin. I watch his head shake curtly.

"Then, I'm not washing anything," I say confidently.

His hold around me loosens, and I slide back to the ground. He takes a step back and my eyes go straight to his proud dick.

"Then, we're done here," Bentley says.

I reach for his shaft. "Doesn't seem that way to me."

He shifts just out of reach. "Wash my chest or leave, Kenzie. Those are your only two options."

Fuck. Why do I find his demands so hot? I want to reject the command, but damn, it doesn't matter that I already had one of the biggest orgasms of my life. I haven't had my fill of this officious man.

Bentley reaches for the condom, and he's less than a second from removing it from his still-hard cock when I grab on to his wrist.

"You're being a man-child, but fine, I'll wash the stickiness from my drink off your chest that's not even there anymore."

There's a subtle twitch in his cheek when I speak, but that's the only sign I get that he's not a complete statue.

I reach for the soap dispenser and let just enough to clean his chest drop into my palm. The green liquid smells like the forest, and I take a deep inhale. *Hmmm, delicious.*

Just like the bossy man I'm about to slather with it.

Chapter Four

Bentley

WHEN I BROUGHT KENZIE INTO THE BATHROOM, I wasn't sure what was going to happen. I sure as hell hadn't expected her to start fingering herself in front of me. Brazen doesn't even begin to describe the woman I've unexpectedly brought into my home.

She is stunning until she opens her mouth. Then, she makes me want to bend her over my knee and spank the defiance right out of her.

Though, as she rubs her hands over my chest with the body wash just as I've demanded, I want to fuck her mouth into submission.

Her hand starts to travel further south, and I snatch it. "No."

She cocks a perfectly arched brow at me. "No? What do you mean *no*?"

"I mean I'm done with the shower, and I want to fuck you in the bedroom."

Her cheeks and chest flush. She might be fighting listening to me, but everything about her actions says she loves each command I give.

Kenzie shrugs and exits the shower. She's soaking wet and doesn't bother to take a towel.

If she gets in my bed...

My hand twitches when I move to follow her, grabbing a towel as I go.

When I enter the bedroom, her auburn hair is fanned out over my pillows, likely destroying the silk fabric.

I stalk forward and grab her ankles, jerking her to the edge of the bed. "You have shit for manners."

I may not like a showy lifestyle, but I still enjoy nice things, and I'm not okay with them being ruined by carelessness.

Still, as much as I want to be angry with the vixen of a woman and kick her out, I decide to fuck the apology I want out of her.

Kenzie is propped up by her elbows watching me intently with bright hazel eyes. She isn't shy with her body, either, pushing her chest out, waiting for me to make my next move.

Instead of letting her get joy out of observing me, I flip her over and bring her hips back until my condom-covered dick presses against her ass.

She makes soft mewling noises and I spread her cheeks apart with my fingers, then slowly trail my hands down until I reach her swollen folds.

Kenzie pushes against my touch, and I pull my hand away.

She looks back at me with narrowed eyes, and I give her nothing in return other than a dead stare. She thinks she knows me, but she doesn't know shit. I'm going to show her that.

As much as I want to drive my dick into her heat, and I'm certain that's what she wants as well, I change my mind and flip her back over without making eye contact with her. Before she can question my motives, I drop to my knees and drape her legs over my shoulders.

One finger rubs against her clit, and my mouth covers the rest of her pussy. She rocks against my face, and I use my free hand to press over her stomach and keep her as still as possible.

My tongue laps at her center, and she thrashes on the bed.

I add another finger and curl them inside her. I expect her to cry out, and when she does, she also tenses under my hold.

She's like putty in my hands, but I'm not ready to give her a release. Not when she carelessly came to lay in my bed.

My head backs up and I wipe my fingers on the towel I dropped to the ground. When I stand back up, she's glaring at me. "That was rude."

"So was getting into my bed without drying off," I deadpan.

She huffs and opens her mouth to say something else, but I'm done hearing her talk. I take a step back and glance down at my cock before looking back up at her.

Kenzie's tongue darts out and she's moving off the bed without me even having to say anything. I take the condom off, and once she's on her knees, I grip her hair with both hands. The moment her lips cover the head, I jerk my hips forward and feel the back of her throat.

To her credit, she doesn't choke or back away. Instead, she bobs and swirls her tongue like my dick is the most delicious thing she's ever tasted.

My chin drops to my chest, and a rumble builds in my chest while I watch her ravish my cock. Her hot little moans vibrate along my shaft and straight to my balls that are tightening by the second.

I loosen my grip on her hair and groan when she takes me deeper than before.

Hell, I'm not going to last long enough to fuck her if I let her continue.

A few more strokes and licks later, I bend forward to grab her shoulders and my dick pops out of her mouth like a fucking lollipop.

She's smiling proudly, but I ignore her smirk and toss her back onto the bed before reaching into my nightstand for another condom. This time I cover myself and stalk back to the mattress.

Kenzie is close to the edge, and I grab her hips before driving my dick into her pussy without warning.

Her head slams back onto the soft surface beneath her and she seems to be struggling to breathe between the loud moans while her nails dig into my comforter.

"Again," she begs.

I'm tempted to deny her, but I don't. Though, I'm not sure if that's more for her benefit or mine.

My hips thrust forward, and I bring her legs up, so that they're both resting on my right shoulder. Her body matches the movements, and I don't slow my pace.

"So close," she murmurs, and I've barely gotten started. She's not making it easy to torture her, but I won't give her the release she's hoping for again. Not yet, anyway.

I pull out of her, and my eyes catch the rising of her open palm, but I'm flipping her back onto her stomach before she can take a swing at me.

"You're being a di—" Her words are cut off when her face meets the mattress. I waste no time pushing her further onto the bed and crawling up myself. I spread her legs apart and lift her hips just enough to slam inside of her again.

My balls tighten. This time, I just might let her come, but only if she stays quiet.

I lean forward, placing a palm between her shoulder blades and grabbing a fistful of hair. My thrusts are slow yet consistent, testing just how mouthy she wants to be.

When she says nothing, I quicken my movements and press more of my weight over her body. Her skin is on fire and burning into my own. It's supple and soft when I trace a finger up her ribs, and she shudders from my touch.

"Please, Bentley," she begs.

Now, she's getting the picture.

I flex my ass and drive harder into her, bringing her hips higher up and deepening the impact of my dick.

"Fuck. Yes. Right there. Jesus. Do not stop, for the love of all that is good in the world." Her words fuel me this time instead of driving me mad.

Kenzie's ass is pressing hard against my hips. She's not letting me get too far away, and I can't say I'm surprised.

"Oh, God." Her forehead pushes into the bed, and she

tightens so hard around my cock that I can't stop my own release while also wondering if there might be bruises later.

I'm coming right alongside her, enjoying the full body shudders overcoming her beneath me.

Her face is hidden by her hair and the comforter. I pull the strands back and make sure she's not suffocating, then pull out abruptly from her still-contracting pussy.

She makes a *harumph* sound when I walk back into the bathroom, and I grin only when I know she can't see.

Kenzie isn't someone I would have ever picked out of the crowd, but she at least wasn't disappointing, and the sex is just what I needed to get past the delirium I blame on jet lag.

I dispose of the filled condom and grab a washcloth to clean myself up. Once I'm done, I grab another towel and wrap it around my waist.

Kenzie is still lying face down on my bed when I return. I give her ankle a shake. "Time to get up."

She groans. "Can't."

"Oh, yes, you can. I need to sleep, so you need to leave." I don't see the point in niceties. She got what she wanted, and so did I. Now, it's time for the evening to be over.

Her eyes snap up and glare daggers at me. "Are you kicking me out? After that?"

"No, I'm telling you to leave on your own accord, so that I don't *have* to kick you out. I'll call you a ride to take you home." I turn for the bathroom to grab the clothes I left in there. When my back is to Kenzie, a pillow hits me in the head.

"You're a dickass," she says, then I hear her get out of bed.

Before I can grab my pants to find my phone, she's in front of me and shoving me out of the bathroom. "I'll get my own damn ride."

She slams the door in my face, and I grin again. I thought I might regret this night, but maybe I won't.

I hear the slamming of drawers and cabinets. "Or maybe I still will," I murmur to myself.

I'm settled into bed by the time Kenzie exits the bathroom. "I assume you can show yourself out?"

She scoffs. "I assume you can go fuck yourself."

She spins on one heel, and I watch her round ass sashay out the door. Her feet stomp down the stairs, echoing through the quiet house. The locks turn, and I hear her mutter something before slamming the door closed on her way out.

"Well, that was fun." I decide to wait several minutes before getting out of bed to lock up behind her.

I sit up in bed so that I don't fall asleep while the time ticks by. The room is now deathly quiet, and I don't like the emptiness that returns.

I'd headed out to work, because I thought it was a good idea. I went to that bar, because I didn't want to be in this house alone.

After bringing Kenzie into it, I'm even more uneasy about the quietness closing in around me.

I give my head a shake. No, this has nothing to do with that vixen and everything to do with the fact that I've just gotten home from a three-month stay in a foreign country. Plus, the lack of sleep.

I'm certain that after a good night's rest and my first day at a new job that I'll feel more like myself again.

I have to. There are people who depend on me. Like my sister, the workers of the shelter I'm on the board for, and now the thousands of employees at West-to-East, Inc. I can't be anything other than perfect and in control.

Not now and not ever.

Chapter Five

PROPERLY FUCKED

Kenzie

THE NEXT MORNING, I'M STILL FUMING ABOUT that prick. He'd given me two of the most overwhelming orgasms that I've ever had, while also getting off himself, and then just kicks me out? Hell fucking no.

I'm already plotting all the things I can do to him while I'm driving to work the next morning. Like toilet papering his house. I'm sure his ritzy-ass neighbors would *love* that. The thought also occurs to me that I could follow him one morning to his work and go in there screaming about the disease he gave me.

The idea of that being recorded and ending up viral gives me a little hesitation. But only a tiny bit. It's still a contender.

I pull into the parking lot of Global Tech and straighten the collar of my nicest blouse. I've never dressed for the job I wanted, mostly because I didn't even realize I wanted a promotion until I got one.

I'd been content with my programming role, but that isn't what living life is about. Contentment is for the boring, and I'm anything but boring.

My heels click against the asphalt, and my dress pants swish around my ankles. The closer I get to the building, the more I'm regretting my wardrobe choice. The dressy clothes might be a bit too much too soon, but it's too late to change now.

I head up to my desk. When I arrive, there's a note for me on my keyboard. Glen rolls his chair over while I read it.

"Clara dropped that off ten minutes ago. Why does Joslin want to see you two days in a row?" he asks.

I shrug without looking at him. "Just work stuff."

I take a step away, and he eyes my outfit. "Are you interviewing for a position I don't know about?"

"Nope." My answer is the truth. I didn't even have to go through hours of tortuous meetings, and that alone makes me smile as I head toward Joslin's office.

My toes are already feeling squished in the new heels, but I keep my stride even and nod at Clara when I arrive. "Is the boss free?"

Clara frowns. "She just got on a conference call that will last a few hours, but she left this for you."

Joslin's assistant hands me a manila folder. I peek inside and see a dozen or more papers. "Thank you."

"You're welcome. Email me if you have any questions. If I don't have the answer, I'll make sure Joslin reaches out by the end of day. That should be the last of the paperwork you need to go through for the new position," she says. I thank her before walking away.

I tuck the packet under my arm and go back to my desk.

Glen is still watching me, and he's whispering something to Peter whose cubical is on the other side of him.

I ignore their pointed stares and take a seat. I log into my computer and pull up my email first. While that loads, I take the papers out and double check Glen isn't standing over me like a creeper.

When I confirm I'm alone, I see the top page labeled "Volunteer Information". It has everything I'll need on the local animal shelter Resolutions. They've been around for decades, and I always see their fundraisers. I'm pretty sure my dad even donated to them a few times over the years, but I've never been to the location or one of the functions.

I'm not against animals, so as long as they don't have me picking up shit, then this won't be a bad volunteer gig.

According to the papers Joslin left for me, the board is having a meeting tomorrow with the other volunteers, and they'd like me present. As I continue to read, I scratch at my neck, annoyed by the collared shirt.

The rest of the documents are for my acceptance of the new position as a project manager. When my eyes spot the salary again, my grin grows, and I'm reminded why I dressed up today.

I will buy all the damn dress pants for this motherfucking position.

Sure, I wasn't a broke ass before this, but my raise will mean a bigger place to live and more freedoms. Like splurging on weekend getaways and saving for the bigger things, like a new car when I need one.

My father always instilled in me to work hard. I want to call him to tell him about the promotion, but I don't know when it will go public within the office. I'll have to wait until I'm off work to let him know.

A text pops up on the screen of my phone, and I smile when I see it's in our group chat.

Ella: How's our girl feeling today? Hopefully a little bow-legged?

I didn't tell them that I was kicked out. I'd only sent a text after midnight to let them know I was still alive and home safely. I'd had enough embarrassment for one night.

Me: Your girl is all good. No cowboy walk for me today.

Piper: Uh oh. She's not dishing about all the dick she had. He must have been bad.

Oh, how I wish she was right.

Instead, I'm pressing my thighs together just thinking about how amazing Bentley was. I only keep that information to myself because I don't need them asking too many questions when I know I'll never see him again.

Me: He wasn't bad or good. It doesn't really matter, though. It was a one-night stand.

Ella: Right. Just like my fiancé was only supposed to be pretend on vacation.

She might be right about her situation, but I'm nothing like Ella. She's strong and beautiful and kind and caring. I'm wild and fire and too much to handle for most men.

My mouth never knows when to shut up, but I learned a long time ago to love myself just the way I am. If I have to change for someone to care about me, then they aren't worth my time.

Piper: Kenzie settle down? I find that hard to

picture... I look forward to meeting the man who can tame our girl, though.

I laugh at that. I know Piper speaks only from the heart.

Me: I love you both. I need to get some shit done. Chat later.

I put my phone down and go back to looking over the papers. Before I get too buried in them, I check my new emails.

Joslin sent one about ten minutes ago, and I click on that first.

McKenzie,

I talked with Marcy in HR. She said they'll post your promotion along with the other restructuring I mentioned on the internal website tomorrow. Since you might not be here when that happens, I wanted to give you a heads up. When you come in on Thursday, you'll be working in your new office. We really want to get things running smoothly with our new workflow as soon as possible, and there are several new projects coming that we need you to get started on right away. Hopefully, you won't be needing any time off in the coming months, but let me know right away if that's something we need to prepare for.

Lastly, don't worry about your desk. All of your items will be transferred to your new office by one of the techs. If you have any issues or questions with the additional paperwork left for you, let me know.

Joslin Croft

A wide grin spreads across my face, and a lightness fills my chest. I might have had the most amazing, yet worst one-night stand ever, but the more I learn about my new role, the more eager I am to get started.

I just hope it's not Glen who has to move my stuff...

With that thought, I put some of my personal items into my purse. I can handle my computer being fucked with, but not the picture of me and my dad or me with my best girls.

I respond to Joslin's email. As long as this volunteer position doesn't require more time from me than I'm expecting, then I don't foresee the need for any days off in the coming weeks or months.

After that, I go through the rest of the papers, keeping my chair positioned just right so I can see if anyone approaches me while I'm going over them.

The rest of the day goes by quickly. I keep my head down and focus on the smaller, lingering projects I had left for my current position and even stay later to get the last one wrapped up.

When I head out to my car, I'm still grinning, even though it's nearing dark and only a few other vehicles are still in the parking lot.

Instead of heading home, I drive to Piper's house. She might still be working, but after the last two days, I need some girl time. Badly. Plus, she's least likely to turn me away now that Ella has Owen to keep her evenings occupied.

I punch in the code for the door lock—something all of us have to each other's houses—and let myself in.

Piper's humming can be heard coming from her office, so I head that way. When I get to the doorway, I realize she must have her earbuds in, because her head is bobbing while her chin rests in her hand.

Her deep-blue eyes are covered by her square-framed glasses, and her gaze scans the computer screen in front of her without noticing me. Her brunette hair is down, falling straight around her circular face and ending past her shoulders. She's wearing a sweatshirt two sizes too big and black yoga pants that remind me I failed to do my morning exercises today. I'll have to make up for it tonight once I'm home.

Piper snorts at something she reads, then types on the keyboard, making me grin. My girl is a kickass editor, and I'm so damn proud of her. Though, we don't talk about her job much anymore. Not when it's going to be taking her away from us.

Deep in my heart, I'm happy for her. But the perpetual five-year-old inside of me is still kicking and screaming while we wait for her final move date to be announced.

I step forward, and she still doesn't see me. I'm creeping slowly, trying not to scare her, but I fail. When I'm right behind her computer screen, Piper screams and picks up her mouse, chucking it right at my face and hitting me in the forehead

"Motherfucking hell, Pipe!" My hands cover my head in case she wants to throw anything else.

"Shit, Kenzie. You scared the hell out of me." I hear her chair creak, and then a second later, her hands are tugging at my elbows. "Let me see."

I lower my arms, and she winces. "It shouldn't bruise, but there's a red mark right in the middle of your forehead. Sorry."

I chuckle. "Are you really?"

She shrugs. "Mostly. What are you doing here? Is everything okay?"

My head nods toward the kitchen. "Do you have some time for a glass of wine? After last night, I thought stopping by here would be safer than the bar."

Piper loops her arm through mine. "Tell me everything." Then, she cringes. "Well, not *everything*."

My body shakes with laughter. "You're no fun."

We step into her hallway, and two turns later, we're in her kitchen. I jump onto the counter, letting my legs dangle over the edge. As Piper gets two glasses and a bottle of wine out, I begin rattling off everything that's happened in more detail than text had allowed, from my promotion to the old lady Louise that I met in the bar, then to Bentley.

She remains stoically silent until I'm finished. Only then does she drink the rest of her wine in one long gulp and begin to fan herself.

"Damn, Kenz. I knew you were wild, but that sounds like a night of passion straight out of the novels I edit." Then, she frowns. "Except for the part where he kicked you out. Neither of you got the other's phone number?"

"Nope," I say with an extra pop at the end.

She levels her eyes on me. "What are you going to do?"

I smirk and rub my hands over my thighs. "What do you mean?"

Piper fills both of our glasses again. "I've known you since grade school, McKenzie Jane. Don't for one second pretend you don't have a plan."

My fingers drum over my dress pants while I lean back against the upper cabinets. "Honestly, I haven't put a ton of thought into anything specific just yet. The work stuff has taken up a lot of brain space. I could just let this go and be thankful for finally getting properly fucked."

She raises a brow. "Or?"

"Or I could figure out a way to cross paths with him again and make his life hell for being such a dick to me." My smirk is all evil. While this idea seems most appealing in the moment, I'm slowly realizing that I deserve better than a good roll in bed.

I deserve to be wanted and cherished and admired for my flaws *and* perfections.

Not kicked out after his dick goes soft.

Maybe I will let this go. Maybe this is my chance to turn over a new leaf.

I have my new position at work, I'll hopefully be getting a new house soon thanks to the pay increase, and yeah...

Fuck Bentley Businessman.

He can kiss my sweet ass. He's the one missing out on greatness, not me.

Chapter Six

MAN CANDY

Bentley

IT'S MY SECOND DAY AT WEST-TO-EAST, INC., AND I'm doing my best to stifle my bad mood. I continue trying to blame it on jet lag even though I've been back in the states for three days now. In reality, I know it's because, even after changing my sheets and pillowcases, I'm still reminded of Kenzie being in my home, which has made my sleep fitful.

She left a strawberry scent behind in my room, and it doesn't matter which way I turn my head, I haven't been able to stop picturing her mouth on my dick every time I close my eyes. Hell, tonight I'm tempted to sleep in one of the guest rooms to see if that helps.

Even as I read an email and wait for the next employee to show up, that woman is on my mind, which is the last thing I want. She was only supposed to be a fuck to take the edge off. Especially after being in a third world country for three months and not touching a woman there because I didn't need anything complicated to distract me when I was supposed to be focused on helping others.

The only positive thing over these last two days has been that all of the employees are welcoming of a stranger being at the helm of their company. The board cautioned me that there may be an adjustment period, but so far, I've met almost all of the department heads and several of the managers beneath them. Each one seemed eager to learn what I was bringing to the table.

My next meeting is with Owen Porter. He's the VP of Marketing and the one I'm most interested in talking with. Marketing is what this company needs to fix the mess left behind from the old CEO. I did my fair share of research before officially taking the job. The guy was selfish in his acquisitions and harsh to the employees affected.

That won't be the way we do things around here anymore. Not if the board wants to see positive, long-lasting growth for this company.

I glance around the office. Fake plants have been brought in and placed around the room, the east wall is all glass with a calming view of the city, and there is a mostly empty bookshelf on the west wall. I intend to rectify that with items from my personal library.

My hands move over the smooth, black surface of the desk, and I lean back in my leather chair. With little effort, I spin until I'm facing the window. I didn't think Charlotte was where I'd put down roots after moving here from New York, but looking out over the city now, I can't see myself anywhere else.

A knock on the door interrupts my thoughts, and I stand. The handle turns before I can open the door myself, and in walks a man about my age with dark, short hair, a crisp charcoal suit with a light green tie.

"Mr. Abbott? I'm Owen Porter from Marketing," he says, keeping his head up. His blue eyes meet my gaze straight on.

I extend my hand, and his grip is sure. "Call me Bentley. It's nice to officially meet you."

He laughs. "You're the only reason I'm still here, so the pleasure is all mine."

My brow raises as we take seats, me behind my desk and him directly across from me. "How so?"

"I used to be one of Jack's executive assistants. I wasn't his biggest fan as the years passed," Owen says, his voice lowering with disdain.

I nod and sit up straighter in my chair. "From what I've heard, I don't blame you. Seems as if your patience paid off, though."

He pulls at the end of his tie. "Almost didn't, but yeah, it's been nice seeing this company take steps in the right direction."

"Well, I intend to make those steps turn into leaps with your help. The marketing department is going to play a big role in my plans," I say.

Owen grins. "We're up for the challenge."

"Good. I'll need a few days to reevaluate everything I've learned so far and see where the best place to start is. I do know that branding for the businesses we already own is a priority, and making sure those that have remained forgotten in the dark corners of the corporation finally have the dust cleared from them."

The longer I speak, the more Owen nods, and his eyes

widen. "If I can be forward, that's everything I hoped you'd say. We don't need to expand to grow. At least, not anytime soon."

I lean back and fold my hands over each other. "You can always speak your piece here, Owen. I won't always do what you want, but I promise to do what I truly believe is best for this company as a whole."

He looks toward the window and then back at me while smiling. "My fiancée will be glad to hear that. She's been worried on my behalf since I decided to stay on with the company. She had the misfortune of knowing Jack Harrington and said she wasn't above threatening you if you were anything like him."

I let out a short chuckle. "Threats? She doesn't work here, does she?"

Owen's grin grows. "No, but she did say if you were open to it, I was to invite you to dinner so she could meet you herself. More threats were given about that if I failed to extend the offer after deciding whether you'd be good for the company."

I raise a brow. "Does your invite mean you believe I'll be just that?"

He nods. "The other department heads have been talking. So far, you haven't given us a reason to think otherwise. We're thankful to have you here."

Out of all the VPs I've met today, he's the first one to be open with me and talk to me more as an equal than someone he needs to fear. Maybe it wouldn't be so bad to form some tighter relationships with those I'll be working the closest with.

"You know what? Tell your fiancée I said yes to dinner.

I'm busy the rest of the day, but any evening this week should work."

His mouth pops open slightly before he recovers. "Oh. Well, okay. I'll let you get back to things and confirm the day and time later tonight."

Owen stands, and I follow him to the door. I give his hand another firm shake. "Thank you for coming by, Owen. I look forward to all the good we can do for West-to-East together."

Owen's grip tightens slightly before he nods and releases. "As do I."

Once he's gone, I glance at the clock. I need to head out for a meeting. It wasn't ideal for this to be scheduled during my first week at a new company, but I have a lot to think about for work. A break after all the meetings I've had should help me process things easier.

I head out of the office after sending a quick email to those I met with today, thanking them again for their time. Same as I did for the others yesterday. My niceties don't mean that I'll be taking things easy on them, but I believe in building a foundation of respect with my employees before demanding their greatest work. If they don't hold me in a positive regard, I won't ever get their best.

My Range Rover is parked in the front row in a designated parking spot. As soon as I'm inside, I let out a quiet snarl. "Kenzie."

The vents blow her sweet scent around me, and I grip the steering wheel tightly while exiting the parking lot.

I'll need to have the house cleaner come early and take my car in for a detail. I can't let another woman distract me. Especially not a mouthy one like Kenzie.

Sure, she was better in bed than I expected, but I don't have it in me to handle *all* of her. I don't need to have gotten to know her well to see that she's bright where I'm dark. That she lives life too chaotically for my organized preferences. Too much time with her could unravel years of my own hard work making sure I was nothing like my parents.

When I pull into Resolutions—the animal shelter that I've been on the board at for three years now—the sound of dogs barking brings a smile to my face. I don't own any pets. Not because I don't love them, but because it wouldn't be fair.

I spend every other summer in a different country. I work long hours. I live alone. No, I'd rather spend my spare time helping a company like this that finds abandoned pets the proper homes to give them a better life than the needle they might get at the pound thanks to overcrowding.

I hop out and head inside. We're meeting today to discuss the annual fundraiser. I haven't caught up on emails yet to know what their plans are looking like so far, but I do intend to write a check and help on the day of. Doesn't sound like a lot, but I do my best. The new job wasn't expected, and my time will be even more limited than past years.

The building is an old house I'd bought and donated to the shelter. It's still within city limits, but there's an acre of property and we've done a lot to take advantage of every square inch. Cats hang out in the windows, sometimes drawing people in, but most of the time, just soaking in the sun.

The yellow paint and white trim are soft instead of

obnoxious, and the flower beds are well cared-for by the other volunteers.

When the bell rings just inside the door, I'm greeted by a few more deep barks and the sound of Joyce calling out. "Be right there."

Joyce has been running this place for decades. She's like the mother I was never blessed with. That woman could ask me for anything, and I'd give it to her.

"Oh, Bentley! You made it home," she says as she comes around the corner. I take steps forward to greet her, and when her surprisingly strong arms wrap around me, the air whooshes right out of my lungs.

"I told you I would," I say with a laugh.

She pulls back and inspects me. Her curly silver hair is bouncing at her shoulders as she nods her head. Her bright green eyes shine, making it easy to ignore the new wrinkles she's taken on since I last saw her.

"Well, we have much to discuss. I was just coming out to lock the door and put up a sign so we can get started."

Joyce sidesteps me and grabs a white piece of paper from the front desk. It's already written on with a long piece of tape secured to the top. Her hand slaps against the clear window on the main door and she turns back to me. "Ready?"

Her grin is infectious, and I return it. "Absolutely."

She heads down the right hallway, her flower, ankle-length skirt swishing as she goes. "We finished the remodel of the back wing this summer. I'll take you back there if you have time after the meeting. We also have a lot of the tasks planned for the fall fundraiser. We just need to assign roles. A few volunteers have moved on this summer, so I brought in a new one, and I'm hoping to get the workload dispersed amongst the rest of us."

I fight back a groan while I read between the lines. Joyce is giving me a fair warning that writing a check might not be enough this time.

"You know I just started at that new company this week, right?" I ask.

She glances back at me and brushes a stray curl out of her eyes. "I'm well aware of what you're up to, Bentley."

My shoulders tense. I'm not sure her tone bodes well for me, but I dismiss it as we enter the meeting room. Though, it's more of a food storage space with a table in the middle of all the bags and cans stacked against the white walls.

Joyce grabs my arm and points to the people around the table. "Just a refresher for everyone before we get started. The man candy on my arm is Bentley Abbott. On my left is Sandy, then Charlie, Sam, Dakota, Mary, Gene, and our newest recruit just joining us today, McKenzie."

My eyes land on the back of the head to the last member. She's not looking at me like the rest. In fact, she's staring pretty hard at her twisting fingers, and her red hair seems all too familiar.

I clench my jaw, burning my gaze into the back of her head, but she refuses to glance up. There's no way it's not her. *Kenzie.*

Joyce gives me a little shove. "Have a seat."

She shuffles past me and takes the chair at the head of the table. The only remaining spot is directly across from this McKenzie.

I try to allow a small hope that this is just a coincidence

and she's not the same woman that I brought into my house, but when I move past her and get a fresh whiff of strawberries, my hands turn into fists while I attempt to keep my face neutral.

I take my seat, and that small sliver of hope I had is set on fire. "So, how long has *Kenzie* been volunteering here?" The disdain is clear in my voice. Then again, I didn't try hard to hide it thanks to my shock at seeing this particular woman here.

Kenzie's lips thin, and her hazel eyes finally land on me, but she keeps her mouth shut as Joyce answers. "Her boss is my daughter who knew we needed help. Let's make sure we all help her feel welcome and that we don't scare her away on the first day."

Joyce's foot finds my shin when she's done speaking, and I let out a soft grunt. Snarky old woman. She's lucky I have all the respect for her.

"Of course. What's first on the agenda?" I ask, my tone now filled with the professionalism I should have had before.

I've faced worse under more uncomfortable circumstances. I can handle this woman for a little while longer.

At least, that's what I tell myself as I do my best not to give Kenzie any more attention than I need to.

Chapter Seven

USED VIBRATOR

Kenzie

LIFE GIVETH AND THEN IT TAKETH AWAY. I GOT A promotion, then had nobody to celebrate with. I got that good fuck I've been looking for, then got kicked out right afterward. I got to meet Joyce and was truly excited about being a volunteer for the animal shelter, then Bentley walked in.

Out of all the motherfucking places I could see him again, it had to be here. Had to be the one place I couldn't tell him exactly what I thought of him no matter who was around.

I didn't realize that the shelter was run by Joslin's mother until after Joyce introduced herself. That meant anything I did was going to get back to my work, and I couldn't afford to fuck up my new role when I hadn't even really gotten started yet.

Bentley is directly in my line of sight, and I decide I need to pretend leaving his house the other night was my idea. I can't let him interfere with my life any more than he already has.

Not even when my thighs squeeze tighter together in an attempt to ease the throbbing I feel when I watch his talented tongue as he speaks.

Joyce slides a stack of papers my way. "Take a page from the top and pass them down, please."

I do as she asks, and she continues speaking.

"This sheet outlines all of the ideas that we've approved for the fundraiser. We will be hosting a carnival right here at the shelter. It will begin at 11am and run until 9pm, so plan on being here all day on October 25th. Our aim is to draw the parents with kids in during the daylight hours and appeal to the adults in the evening. More importantly, our goal is to find proper homes for at least half of the animals we have on the day of the event."

The balding man I think is Sam points at the top line. "How are the eight of us going to keep this running smoothly for the whole day with all of the booths we decided on?"

Joyce grins. "Well, I'm hoping our new volunteer can help fill a few spots with new blood. My daughter said she would also try to send a few more people our way. Plus, we all have a friend or two that might help for the day as long as we do the heavy lifting, yeah?"

Heads nod, including mine. "I have a couple friends I know will help."

Ella and Piper love stuff like this, and I can always count on them when I give them plenty of notice. Unlike the other night when I wound up in *his* bed.

Shit. Not going there. We had great sex. It's over now.

I'm an adult, and I need to handle this situation with maturity while remembering the mindset I had when I was at Piper's. I deserve better than the way Bentley treated me, which means I need to forget about him.

Right, a little voice in my head draws the word out.

I ignore my subconscious and focus on the rest of the meeting. The sheet of information is confirmed and locked in. The next thing we need to do is assign jobs.

"I've already put some thought into this, and we'll be here all day if everyone tries to pick their own, so I've grouped you together in pairs of two. You'll each have one or two responsibilities. If something truly doesn't work for you, please see me afterward so the rest of us can get back to our busy schedules."

Nobody objects to Joyce's decision, and I'm realizing now that she probably doesn't get told "no" very often. She's too grandmotherly for anyone to *not* want to please her.

Names and assignments are rattled off. I realize too late that one name in particular hasn't been said. At least not until it's combined with mine.

"McKenzie and Bentley, the two of you will be in charge of donations, some of the rental equipment that we'll need the day of, and catering. I assume with your corporate experience that the two of you will already have connections you can reach out to?"

I'm too stunned to talk. I can't be partnered with Bentley. Give me the sleepy-looking Gene or furrowed-brow Mary. Anyone other than Bentley.

He nods. "Of course, Joyce. Whatever you need."

She pats his hand. "I knew I could count on you. Plus,

you've been here longest, so I need you to help McKenzie get settled in." Then, she swivels to meet my shocked eyes. "This might be a little overwhelming, but I promise, you're in good hands with Bentley. He's not like most suits that you'd meet."

I bark out a laugh that I try to cover with a cough. Thankfully, the other volunteers are getting up, and the scratching of chair legs over the laminate floors helps to distract from my inappropriate outburst.

Joyce tilts her head toward me. "Are you okay?"

I lamely give her a thumbs up. "Right as rain."

She stands up as she says, "Good. We're excited to have you part of the team. If you enjoy this event, maybe we can make you part of the board as well. Currently, we're full, but I know Mary is ready for less responsibilities around here. She's our treasurer. You any good with money?"

I fold the paper with the event information in half and tuck it into my purse before getting up from my chair and answering her.

"I'm good with numbers and computers, so I'm sure I can be good with money, too."

Joyce pats my shoulder. "Joslin chose well for me. I warned her not to send me anyone who wasn't up for a challenge." Her eyes rove over me. "You've got good bones."

Then, she just walks away.

Well, that was the weirdest compliment I've ever received. At least, I think it was a positive comment.

I turn for the door, intent to ignore the way Bentley has been staring daggers at me ever since I began chatting with Joyce, but he isn't having any of that.

"McKenzie." His voice is deep and low, and the irritation I'm sensing from him makes a grin rise on my face while I twist around.

"Yes, Bentley?"

His hands press down on the table, and he leans forward as if he means to intimidate me. "Did you know who I was before you spilled your drink on me?"

I keep my smirk and trail my gaze over his chest and toward his hips since the rest of him is hidden behind the table. "No."

"So, it's just a freak coincidence that you're the new volunteer at the only place in Charlotte that I freely give my time to?" His cheek has this lovely twitch in it that I decide I like.

I shrug. "Seems so. Now, I don't expect you to teach me anything. I'll figure out what I need to know on my own, but I do expect you to pull your weight with these assignments. I can handle the—"

A resounding snarl cuts me off. "Resolutions means a lot to me. You're not going to fuck this up. You're going to take everything we do here seriously. More importantly, we're going to pretend the other night never happened."

I rest my hands over the table, copying his movements, only mine aren't full of anger. They're relaxed and confident. Bentley might think he knows me, but I've watched my father in his lawyer element. Showing emotions never works well for anyone.

"You're right about all of that, Bentley," I say sweetly, then add, "Whatever disappointment we shared can be our little secret. A mistake to never be spoken of again."

He straightens and scoffs. "Disappointment? Right.

Whatever you need to tell yourself to feel better, sweetheart."

"My recently used vibrator says my words are no lie, but that's not important. This event is. And as I was saying before I was rudely interrupted, we'll split the duties. I'll take catering and rentals. You can have donations. I'll let you know if I have questions or when I'm done. Preferably the latter."

His jaw is wound so tightly that I don't hear anything more than a grumble as his reply.

Considering this a win, I turn sharply on my heel and head toward the front door.

I may have never wanted to think about Bentley Abbott again, but maybe torturing him could be the kind of fun I've been missing in my life.

Chapter Eight

PENIS COOKIES

Bentley

WHEN I GET HOME, ALL I WANT TO DO IS HEAD FOR my gym room, eat, go over a few emails, and sleep. Only when I see my sister's silver Mercedes parked in front of my house, I try not to be disappointed. Especially since it's been three months since I've seen her.

I park in the garage and head inside. She has a key, so I don't suspect she's waited in her car for me to get home.

"Celia?" I call as I walk through the kitchen.

"Media room," her voice echoes through the sparse house.

As I make my way through the hallways, I try to be grateful that my grandmother left this place to me, but it's much more house than I would have ever bought for myself.

When I enter the media room, Celia is lounging on the long red couch and eating popcorn. She has her dark-blonde hair pulled up in a high ponytail, making her cheekbones look even sharper than normal, and she's still wearing her polo from the bakery and dark-wash jeans.

She doesn't even look back or bother to get up when I clear my throat. "Missed me that much, huh?" I joke and walk around to sit on the couch with her.

While I'm lifting her feet to make room, she raises a finger at me. "This is the best part."

I glance at the screen. It's some sappy romance movie I'm sure she's seen a hundred times. Women. They're odd creatures.

The thought makes an image of Kenzie pop into my head. I close my eyes and lean my head back. How is it possible that my first night back, I fucked the one woman I won't be able to avoid at least for the next eight weeks?

She's crass, loud, unfiltered, wild, and everything I never wanted in a woman.

At first, I blamed the jet lag for my choices, then it was my ex Selene for pissing me off over the phone, but the more I allow myself to think about Kenzie, the more I realize it was the fire in her eyes that challenged me. Made me want to know if I could put out the flames.

Spoiler alert: I failed.

Celia's foot kicks me in the ribs. "My movie is over. Wake up."

I turn my head toward her and open my eyes. "Hello to you, too."

She gets up and moves to lean her head against my chest and drapes an arm over my stomach. "I missed you, big brother."

"I missed you, too, little sister." I squeeze her tightly

against me. "But if you ever tell Selene anything about me again, I'll change the locks."

Celia gasps. "You wouldn't."

I raise a brow. "I would. That woman isn't for me. I don't want to hear from her anymore."

She sighs. "I really am sorry, but I think she's learned from her mistakes. You should give her another chance. She's always so kind to me, and I know she loves you."

Selene is a master manipulator, and I've tried to tell Celia this many times, but unfortunately, Selene hasn't ever slipped up with my sister.

I grab both of her shoulders gently. "Listen, Ce. I know you mean well, but I really am done with her. I'm glad you can keep your friendship, but please don't try and get us back together. It's only going to hurt Selene more."

Just as I hoped, Celia frowns at my last sentence. "That wouldn't be good for any of us. I'll do my best to keep your name out of our conversations." Then, she grins widely. "I have this other friend..."

"Absolutely not." I stand and reach my hand to her. "If you want me to still speak to you and allow you in this house, then you'll leave my love life alone."

Celia rolls her light-blue eyes. "You're no fun now that you're getting gray hairs."

I sneer, pulling her up with a jerk. "I am not."

She laughs and loops an arm through mine. "Come on, you big grump. I brought pizza. It's in the oven."

"How are things over at the bakery?" I ask as we head to the kitchen.

Her smile widens, and her eyes glass over with pride. "Excellent. One of my social media videos went viral, and

I've had almost too many orders to process. Wanna guess what for?"

I groan. "Not really."

She throws her hands in the air. "Penises. All the penis cookies."

Her storefront doesn't sell anything of the sort, but my sister has found her niche online and makes more there than she does right here in Charlotte.

"They have cream-colored—"

My hand quickly covers her mouth. "If you love me like you say, do not tell me what you do with those cookies."

Her entire body shakes, and I remove my hand. "You need to get laid. You're seriously grouchy."

I snort, but say nothing in reply. Getting "laid" has only made my attitude worse.

She pokes a finger into my ribs. "You've only been home for a few days. Did you already meet someone?"

"No." My voice is clipped. We enter the kitchen, and I move to focus on the pizza while Celia gets the plates.

Surprisingly, she doesn't continue to prod at my sex life, and we each grab a couple slices of thick-crust, pepperoni-and-sausage pizza. It's crispy and slightly burnt from the wood-fired oven. Just how I like my pies.

"So, how's the new job?" Celia asks after we've both finished our first piece in comfortable silence.

I wipe the grease from my face and fingers before getting up to grab drinks. "Better than I thought it would be. The employees seem overly excited to have a new CEO."

She accepts the offered water bottle. "From what you told me before, I don't blame them. Are you diving right in with changes or taking things slow?"

I sit back down. "A little of both. Some things are long overdue. Others, I don't know enough about to decide if they should be changed or left alone. I met with all of the VPs, though. They're rather capable, and I'm not overly worried about getting all aspects of the company back into the green."

She nudges me with her elbow and grins. "I can give your marketing team some social media advice."

I shake my head. "Thanks, but no thanks. I'm actually having dinner with the marketing VP and his fiancée this week."

Her jaw pops open. "Look at my big brother making friends for the first time since college. I'm so proud of you."

"I have friends," I say, but the words fall flat, even to me.

The people I went to school with only cared about money, their social standing, and what careers would help with those things. I never fit into that world. Celia did, but she chose to follow me here instead of staying in New York with our parents when I'd finally been pushed to my limits.

It was something I never thought too hard on, because the idea that my little sister was only here to watch over me was depressing.

We finish our pizza and chat about my volunteer work in Peru for a while before she heads home. When I head upstairs for the evening, I eye the door to my home gym, but brush the thoughts away. Tomorrow will be a better day for a workout.

Instead, I grab my work bag and head to my office. A little late-night work to hopefully help me sleep better.

———

THE NEXT TWO DAYS GO BY IN A BLUR OF meetings, projects, and caffeine. I hardly have a moment to think about Kenzie or the carnival we're supposed to be planning together, which, for the latter, isn't good. There are still eight weeks left, but I can't put off getting feelers out for potential donors.

Frustration builds inside me that I'm letting my feelings make this harder than necessary. Still, I don't understand why Joyce partnered me with Kenzie.

I love that woman like family, but sometimes she's too much.

Whatever her reasoning was for giving me this hardship, I need to find a way not to care about the things that shouldn't matter. I don't want to ruin the biggest fundraiser of the year for Resolutions. That's most important to me.

A knock echoes through my office, and the open door swings even further open. I see Owen leaning against my doorframe.

He nods at the piles of paperwork on my desk. "I've never seen so much work being done in this office before."

I chuckle and set my pen down. "Get used to it."

Owen glances at his watch. "Are you going to be finished in time for dinner tonight?"

I peek at the clock on my computer screen. Fuck. It's already after six, and Owen's wife—or whatever she is— planned for seven.

"Yeah, as long as you don't mind me showing up empty-handed and in my work clothes," I say with a shrug.

He waves a hand in the air. "Ella has already prepared way too much food. She's been excited about this all week, and you'll feel like a stuffed pig by the time you leave."

A pang of jealousy rolls through me. "Sounds like you've got yourself one hell of a woman, Porter. I'll see you at seven."

He nods and backs out of the doorway, so I can get back to work. Well, get back to organizing all these damned papers, so I can take them home with me to work late tonight. If I'm going to find time tomorrow to call around for the event, then I'll be up half the night making sure my work here is done first.

———

With only one minute to spare, I pull up to Owen's house. It's a simple home with blue paint, white shutters, and a manicured front yard. There's nothing extraordinary about it, but it's a home filled with two people who love each other, and that's a lot more than I've ever had.

Before my thoughts can get lost in my past, I exit my car and brush my hands over my light-blue dress shirt. I left my suit coat and tie in the back seat, trying to keep things casual since I didn't have time to go home and change.

When I get to the red front door, my knuckles don't get the chance to touch the steel before the hinges creak.

"Sorry. Ella made me come greet you like a stalker," Owen deadpans.

"Owen Joseph Porter, you did not just say that," I hear a woman shrill from somewhere behind him.

Owen leans forward and whispers, "I have no idea why she's freaking out so bad. We have dinner with people all the time. Don't hold this evening against me."

My hand clasps over his shoulder. "Don't worry about it, man."

He moves out of the way and gestures with his hand for me to come in. I step into the foyer and see a living room on my left. Further up is a hallway that I assume leads to the kitchen and dining area. Owen goes that way, and I follow.

The walls are painted a light tan with white crown molding. Pictures adorn the painted surface, but I don't linger.

Behind the kitchen counter, I see who I assume to be Ella grabbing dishes from the stove and getting ready to carry them to the table.

She looks up at me and gives me a wide smile. "Hi and sorry. I'm not usually such a mess. I tried to get everything done earlier, but, well, as you see, that didn't work out."

"Don't even worry about it. Everything smells delicious, Ella. Thank you for inviting me," I say with a smile.

Owen has already gone around to help her. When they deny my offer to assist, I make my way into the small dining area where they're headed with the covered dishes.

Ella sets her items down and glances back up at me. "I made pot roast. I hope that's okay."

My stomach chooses that moment to gurgle. "I think that's your answer."

She laughs and starts to head back to the kitchen.

"Are you sure there isn't anything I can help with?" I ask with my hand on the back of the chair.

Ella shakes her head. "Absolutely. You're our guest. Have a seat. Owen will get you a drink. We've got the three Ws: whiskey, water, or wine."

I look over at Owen who's back in the kitchen. "Whiskey, please."

Before Ella gets any more frazzled, I take a seat in the chair against the window, so I can see them both working together in the small kitchen.

They share slight smiles and touches when they pass each other, and I wonder how different my childhood would have been if I'd had parents who even looked at each other when they weren't required to.

I might have grown up with money, but that was it. Everything else was ice cold except for my relationship with Celia. As much as she drives me crazy, I'm thankful to have her.

Owen and Ella join me at the table. He hands me a glass with two fingers of whiskey in it, and I decide to wait until I've eaten a bit to try it.

"So, Bentley. How are you liking Charlotte so far?" Ella asks as she serves her food first.

"I've lived here for about six years, actually. It's been a nice change from New York City," I answer, hoping she doesn't get too personal with her questions.

Her shoulders shudder. "I went to New York once. Almost died when I was knocked into the street by a group of teenagers. No thanks."

I laugh. "Yeah, it's a special breed of people up there."

Owen takes a sip of his drink, then asks, "Has West-to-East been what you thought it would be so far?"

I'm silently grateful for the business question, but before I can answer, a voice calls out from the front door.

"Ella Rosalynn! You can't keep ignoring me, woman. We have dick to discuss."

My hands curl into fists, and I tilt my head up, wondering what the hell I did to the universe to deserve such bad luck.

Kenzie walks further into the house and laughs once she makes it to the kitchen. The sound is soft at first, then becomes louder and more maniacal.

The floor feels like it's dropped out from beneath me. How can this be happening? *Again.*

Owen pushes his chair back and gets up. "Kenzie, what the hell is wrong with you? This is my boss."

Her wild eyes look around Owen and land on Ella, then Kenzie points to me with a smile too big to be natural or sane. "Well, at least you'll know who I'm talking about from the other night when we finally get to catch up."

Ella gasps, and Owen's head swivels between all three of us.

Fuck.

Chapter Nine

DILDO COLLECTION

Kenzie

ELLA HAD BEEN OUT OF TOUCH, AND GIVEN I hadn't seen her since before I found out about my new job, I'd run out of patience. Which is how I ended up walking into her house to find Bentley sitting at her dinner table.

Clearly, the universe isn't going to let me get away from Bentley Abbott. That is, unless he kills me first. That would do the trick.

Maybe I shouldn't have told Owen and Ella that I fucked his boss as soon as I walked in. That was possibly the wrong move, but sometimes my lips work faster than my brain and I can't help what leaves my mouth.

Now, though, watching Bentley glare daggers at me, I realize that might be something I should work on. At some point.

Ella gets up from the table and pushes Owen back. Yeah, he's also giving me nasty looks. Not surprising when he refused to hook me up with any of his co-workers before.

Ella grabs my hand. "Come with me, Kenzie."

Her tone is even, not boding well for me.

She drags me out the front door and down to my car. "Unlock the doors."

I raise a brow. "Are you sending me away?"

Her head shakes. "No, I want to yell at you without Owen's boss hearing me sound like a banshee."

My fingers dig my keys out of my purse. "Makes sense."

I move around to the driver's seat, and before I even have my door closed, I try to explain. "First, I didn't know who Bentley was when I hit on him at the bar. Secondly, he's a prick. You shouldn't care what he thinks. That bastard kicked me out after we had sex. Thirdly, this all could have been avoided if you'd responded to my texts and calls with a little more than 'I'm busy' or 'Sorry, can't talk' for the last three days."

She barks out a dark laugh. "You're blaming your dick confession outburst on me? That's rich, Kenz. I know you don't like to hold back, but this dinner is important to Owen. I worked really hard on it, and I'd also promised to call you tomorrow. Are you that hung up on Bentley that you couldn't wait to tell me what happened until then?"

Shit. Her tone is too serious. Ella is never mad at me. Not truly. I don't like the knot twisting in my chest, knowing that I've disappointed her.

"I'm sorry, Ella. I didn't mean to screw up your evening. I just needed...I don't even know. It's not important. This week has just been insane and, well, that's no excuse. I'll go home."

I move to put the keys in the ignition, but Ella grabs my wrist. "Thank you for apologizing sincerely. I know I haven't been around much. You got that promotion, and then I didn't realize so much else had happened. So, I'm sorry as well. Why don't we go for a drive, and you can tell me all about it?"

I nibble on my lip. My guilt hasn't gone away just because she's not yelling at me. "It's okay. You go finish your evening with your guest."

Ella chuckles, but the sound is soft and tired. "I think the evening is over. Honestly, I'm glad. I suggested the dinner idea to Owen because, thanks to a few errant comments from me, he started to worry that his new boss was going to be just another dick. Then, when he told me his boss actually said yes to the invitation, I felt so much pressure to make the evening perfect. Blake had never let me help with anything like this, and all my other exes, well, they sucked at life. This evening became a bigger deal in my mind than it should have."

I lean over the center console of my car and rest my head on her shoulder. "It's okay, Ella. Being excited to do 'wifely things' with your soon-to-be husband is nothing to sweep under the rug. You had every reason to make a big deal."

She gives my hand a squeeze, and I look up to find her grinning. "Owen's boss is really the guy you went home with the other night?"

My smirk grows while I move back to my own seat. "Yep."

"And? I know you said you weren't bow-legged, but now I'm beginning to think you just weren't ready to dish on the real details. How was it?"

I groan and nod. "The 'details' were great until he kicked me out."

She gasps and turns further in her seat to face me. "He did not."

"Oh, he did. Then, two days later? I show up at this volunteer thing that I'm required to do for my new position, and guess who is there for the same thing?"

Ella's head is shaking, and her eyes widen. "No way. It was Bentley?"

I nod. "Unfortunately. He acted like he didn't know me, so I did the same thing. And afterward, we agreed to pretend that night never happened, and I fully wanted to do that, but the more I thought about this fucked-up situation, the more I needed to talk it out. I saw Piper the other night, and that helped, but when I saw him again, I figured it was your turn to tell me I'm crazy. Plus, it's not the same without both of you in my head."

Ella's fingers drum over her thigh. "So, you went home with him, had sex, got kicked out, and planned to never see him again, but now you're going to be stuck seeing him because of this volunteer thing? How long does it last?"

I let out a heavy sigh. "It's a carnival fundraiser for the animal shelter downtown called Resolutions. It isn't until October Twenty-Fifth, so at least another eight weeks. Plus, if he's coming over here, I guess I might see him again."

She waves a hand in the air. "Oh, don't worry about here. I'm sure he'll never come to our house again after tonight."

I grimace and apologize. Again.

"Save the 'I'm sorry' for Owen. You're going to be on his shitlist. I'm already over it," Ella says with a slight frown.

"I'll buy you some sexy lingerie. He'll forgive me once he sees you in nothing other than red lace." I waggle my brows and shimmy my chest.

Ella laughs and slaps lightly at my arm. "Right. Well, that might work, but no promises." Then, she nods at the house. "What are you going to do about Bentley?"

I shrug. "That's what I came over here for. Piper said I should forget about him, and I agreed with her, but now, that seems a little impossible."

"Yeah, I can see that. I didn't get to chat with him, so I have no clue what he's like in a private setting, but Owen said he's always professional and patient and willing to listen to the other employees. Maybe you should just kill him with kindness. If you don't give him any more reasons to want to murder you with his eyes, then maybe you can survive this volunteer thing."

My shoulders sag. "I was kinda hoping you'd tell me to go find a new man to screw and to keep pretending none of this happened."

Ella smiles. "Not likely."

My hands scrub over my face for a few seconds while I think. "I can probably find a way to be nice to him if he's not being a dick to me first."

"That's the spirit." She pats my arm.

Voices sound from the front of the house, and even some laughter. Ella and I both look toward the door to find Owen walking Bentley to his Range Rover, which I now see is parked just past the house. In my defense, it's already dark outside and easy to miss a black vehicle.

Their eyes cast our way for the briefest second, and Owen slaps his hand on Bentley's shoulder.

"What do you think they're talking about?" I ask Ella. She chuckles. "You."

I roll my eyes. "Probably. I should go, too. Tell Owen I'm sorry and he'll be getting a package from me soon to strengthen my apology. And remind him that if his boss holds fucking me against Owen, then that has nothing to do with me and all to do with Bentley."

Ella reaches for the door. "That actually makes a lot of sense."

"Of course it does. I said it," I tease.

She gets out of the car and leans back down. "I love you, and I'm sorry I wasn't there this week when you needed me. In the future, maybe just text me the information, so I realize you're not just needing to talk about how you organized your dildo collection by color instead of size."

"That was one time," I yell with a groan when she shuts the door and waves at me through the window.

I blow her a kiss and see that Owen is waiting for her by the front door with a wistful look on his face. He really is perfect for my best friend. Hopefully, he won't stay pissed at me for long.

The taillights to Bentley's SUV light up, and he revs the engine before turning around in the street. I stare at his tinted windows until he passes, wondering if he was looking at me, too.

Pathetic? Maybe.

Do I care? Absolutely not.

Chapter Ten

BLUE FUCK-ME HEELS

Bentley

A fresh start. That's what I thought I was getting when I came back from Peru. I wasn't attached to anyone, and I was starting a new job. I just had to go and let my cock fuck everything up.

Kenzie has somehow managed to appear everywhere in my life, and I don't understand how things have spiraled so quickly. Or why I can't get her out of my thoughts.

She walked into Owen's house as if she owned the place, talking about *my* dick. Owen laughed it off, saying Kenzie is the wild one of their group, and he's used to her spouting off. He was being kind, because I'm his boss.

A line was crossed last night that never should have existed in the first place. One I now need to rectify.

Though, I haven't decided just how I want to do that. What I do know is that my work, the shelter, and making sure I don't disappoint either of those places are important to me.

For now, I'm doing my best to push that infuriating redhead from my thoughts and focus on the reports on my desk.

My phone vibrates, and when I glance at the screen, I see Celia's name.

"How's my favorite brother this morning?" she asks when I answer.

I grunt. "Busy."

"That's nothing new. You always find something to occupy your time. We're having lunch. I'm going to be at your work at noon exactly. You're not allowed to say no. This is non-negotiable."

I pinch the bridge of my nose. "What did you do, Celia?"

She scoffs. "I didn't do a damn thing, Bentley. Us hanging out the other night just made me realize how much I missed you this summer."

Fuck. I'm such an asshole sometimes.

"Sorry, Ce. I'll see you for lunch," I say with a softer tone.

"Love you, Brother."

I lean back in my chair. "Love you, too."

When she hangs up, I throw my phone back on the desk and let out a heavy sigh as I turn to look out the windows. The sky is clear, the sun is shining, and I should be happy. But fuck, I'm not.

Even Kenzie's laugh haunts me as I sit there and try to sort out my thoughts. I need to figure out what the hell I'm going to do about this insane woman.

My desk phone rings, and I swivel back to answer it to see my new assistant's name. "Hello, Brad."

He chuckles, and my annoyance rises.

He clears his throat. "Sir, a Miss Kenzie Chase is here to see you."

"You've got to be fucking kidding me." I growl into the phone.

"I heard that," she shouts from the hallway.

I slam the phone down and storm across my office. With more than necessary force, I jerk my door open, point at her, then into my office.

Her arched brow quirks up. "Would you like me to come...in, Bentley?"

"Don't show up at my work and play games," I respond with as even of a tone as I'm currently capable of.

Brad shrinks back into his chair and finds something very interesting about a notepad on the desk.

Kenzie sighs and waltzes forward. When she passes me, she flicks hair over her shoulder that hits me in the face.

The rumble in my chest isn't quiet. Damn it. I wasn't ready to see her again. I needed to sort out my thoughts, but here she is, dressed in a sleek black dress, blue fuck-me heels, and a matching three-button coat that she tosses onto one of the chairs in front of my desk.

Her hands slide over her sides before she takes a seat in the remaining spot, then looks back at me, her hazel eyes roaming over my body. "Are you going to stand over there the entire time I'm here?"

I shut the door with minimal effort. I don't need the employees hearing me slam doors.

I take calming breaths and stay quiet until I'm seated behind my desk. Kenzie's uninvited appearance has given me an idea, one that just might be exactly what I need to tolerate these next couple of months.

With my emotions in check, I lean back in my chair and fold my hands lightly over my lap. I don't miss how her eyes dart to my crotch and watch my movements. Yeah, she's still thinking about that night.

Unfortunately, so am I.

"What do I owe the pleasure of this visit, Ms. Chase?" I ask.

Her head cocks to the side, and I know my change in tone has confused the hell out of her. Exactly what I was hoping for.

She crosses her legs, and I fight the desire to look down at her creamy skin.

"I came to discuss the needed items for Resolutions. I've been talking with Joyce since you didn't respond to my earlier emails, and she insisted that I ask you the questions I have. So, here I am." She smirks. "I hope I haven't caught you at a bad time."

I force a smile to my face. "Of course not. I must have missed the emails. What questions do you have?"

She reaches across to her jacket and pulls out a folded piece of paper. The dip at her hips and the way her dress hugs the curve there is hard to miss when she moves like that, but by the time she's looking back up, I'm staring only at her face.

Her finger skims the sheet. "Let's see, I need access to the drive that has the past year's event figures. If I'm going to be reserving the rental equipment, I'll need to be aware of how many people we anticipate showing up."

"Understandable." I slide closer to my desk and start typing while she continues with her "needs" list.

Past records, information on donors I've secured, buffet options or food trucks for the catering options, and insisting I review her list of pros and cons to each.

While I'm a little annoyed with her insistence, I'm also impressed that she's gotten so much done already when I've only made one phone call for donations. I'll have to get Brad to draft an email for me so I can get things going faster.

"Will there be anything else?" I ask when she stops talking to take a breath.

She nods and meets my stare. "I'll need your phone number since your email doesn't seem to take priority. That is, if you'd like any future visits to be planned. Oh, but don't worry about sharing your address. I already have that should I need it."

Her lips twitch, but I don't take the bait. If she's here to discuss business, what happened between us won't be brought up in the conversation. Not if I can help it.

I grab a sticky note and jot down my number before handing it to her.

Kenzie's fingers brush mine, and a shock zaps my skin. An odd noise sounds from her throat, and she quickly pulls away.

"Very well, Mr. Abbott. I guess that covers things, then." She stands and swivels her ass in my direction, then she bends over for longer than necessary to grab her coat.

I clear my throat and stand. "I'll be in touch once I have the other information you need."

She turns back, and her heated eyes roam over me. It

takes every effort not to move when she does. "Sounds excellent."

Kenzie lets herself out of my office, and when the door closes behind her, I glance down at my traitorous dick. "That one is off limits."

When I settle back into my chair, my phone pings with a text from a number not saved in my phone.

Unknown: Thanks for not kicking me out this time. I look forward to making this event a success.

I groan at her mention of "this time".

This woman isn't going to make anything easy on me, and I'm worried my earlier idea of treating her as a business deal won't work.

If I can't scare her away with my fury, fuck her out of my mind, or pretend she's nothing more than a work thing to be dealt with, then what the hell am I supposed to do with Kenzie Chase?

Chapter Eleven

DICKMATIZED

Kenzie

ANOTHER WEEK GOES BY, AND THE ONLY CONTACT I've had with Bentley has surprisingly been through email. He never responded to my text and, while I didn't expect him to, I'm woman enough to admit I was disappointed he didn't take the opening to banter with me.

Polite Bentley isn't nearly as much fun as Fucking Bentley or Furious Bentley. He's this dark cloud that I'm drawn to. Maybe it's because before that night, I'd never been kicked out of someone's house after screwing them. Or it could be because I'm glutton for punishment, but either way, I've decided that I'm not done with Bentley Abbott. Not by a long shot.

Though, tonight isn't about him. It's Friday and, for the first time in much too long, I'm going to have both of my girls with me. Just the three of us.

Between my promotion, the fundraiser, and their own

busy schedules, it's been hell pinning down a time we could hang out, but we finally managed to get our shit together.

I pull up to Piper's house, which is actually just a small two-bedroom guest house at her mother's. I tried to convince her to share a place with me, but the three of us decided nearly a decade ago that we weren't meant to live together. Not after the twelve months of hell that almost cost us our friendships when we turned eighteen.

Piper was smart enough to remember that dark time in our lives and told me in the sweetest tone, "Not a chance in hell."

Before I can get out to go knock on her door, she's already walking my way. Her hair is curled and bouncy, and she's wearing dark skinny jeans with black ankle boots and a dark-red scoop-neck tee.

I roll down the passenger's window and whistle. "Looking good, woman!"

She blushes and pushes her glasses higher up on her nose. "I haven't left the house in days. Working from home isn't what I imagined it would be."

"Why don't you go back to the office if you don't like being home right now?" I ask when she gets in and shuts the door.

Piper sighs. "I'm not even supposed to be in the state still. They gave my desk to the guy who replaced me."

As much as I hate talking about Piper leaving, I know it's important to her. "What's the latest with the move?"

She buckles up, and I start driving while I wait for her to answer.

"I don't know. I guess they got the permits figured out,

but it might not be until December now." She stares out the window, and I reach for her.

"Hey, everything is going to work out. I have my own office now. You could come work in my space," I say.

She laughs, brushing back a few strands of hair. "We'd get nothing done. I think tonight will help get my head back into focus, though. We've all been so busy. I'm not used to *not* seeing you and Ella at least a few times a week. I don't like it."

I frown. "Neither do I. Let's make sure it doesn't happen again."

She looks over at me, a bright look in eyes. "You're the one that's good at threats. I'll leave you in charge of that task."

I mean, she's not wrong. At least when it comes to my friends. I don't waste threats on useless people. Like Bentley.

Shit. I don't want to think about him while I'm supposed to be enjoying the time with my best girls.

"Whoa. What did the steering wheel do to you?" Piper asks.

My knuckles are nearly white from my frustrations. "Nothing. Like you said, it's just been a stressful couple of weeks."

Her head tilts back. "But not tonight. We're going to get drunk and eat all the junk food and forget about all the things."

I loosen my grip. "I'll drink to that."

We pull up to Ella's, and I park in the driveway. Owen is supposed to be gone for the night. I don't know where he went or why, and I don't care. All I know is I get my girls without interruption.

Piper and I walk up to the door where Ella greets us with three bottles of wine in her arms. "Welcome ladies!"

Her grin is wide and has my own growing. I hug her before stealing a bottle. "I assume you're sharing?"

Ella nods and hands one to Piper before hugging her as well. "Absolutely. We're all getting drunk tonight."

I shut the door and follow them into the kitchen where Ella has trays of snacks and more bottles on the counter.

"Look at you, turning into the hostess queen," I joke before grabbing á slice of cheese and salami.

Ella groans. "I know. I don't know what's gotten into me lately. And no, I'm not pregnant. I took a test this morning to be sure before I indulged." She holds up the wine bottle.

Piper nudges her shoulder. "Look at you being extra responsible, too. I thought with your new adrenaline penchant that I was going to have two wild best friends to pretend I'm capable of keeping in line."

Ella barks out a laugh. "If I ever get to Kenzie-level crazy, please smack me."

I throw a piece of cheese at her. "Rude. There is nothing wrong with being like me."

She pulls the food from her long russet hair and tosses it back at me. "Not one bit, but we certainly don't need two of you around here. Unless it's a mini-you, then I'll accept that any day of the week."

My head shakes furiously. "I'd need a man for that to happen."

Piper lifts a brow. "Do you, though?"

Okay, maybe I didn't, but no babies for me. Not yet, anyway.

We each grab a plate of the food and head into the living room with our bottles still in tow. Once we're settled on the couch, Ella looks over at me. "Speaking of men... How are things with Bentley?"

I groan. "I don't want to talk about him tonight."

"Why? I thought he was nice last time you saw him?" Piper asks while she opens her wine bottle.

A chuckle escapes my lips while I pick at my food. "Nice? No, I said professional. There's a difference."

"Well, it's better than him kicking you out and ignoring your questions," Ella says, and I glare at her.

"Thanks for the reminder. I've been trying to forget allowing myself to get dickmatized by that prick." I cross my arms and look up at the ceiling. "His cock really is too good for him."

Ella and Piper are silent for a beat before they both start laughing so hard, I'm afraid they're going to choke.

"You say a lot of funny shit, Kenz, but I think 'dickmatized' takes the crown," Ella finally says while I stare blankly at each of them.

"Maybe I should buy him a coffee mug with the word dickmatizer on it. Maybe he'd laugh enough that the stick shoved up his ass would fall out."

Piper swipes at the few stray tears on her cheeks. "Please do and video it when you give the cup to him."

Honestly, it's not a terrible idea.

When they finally calm down, Ella reaches for me. "I'm sorry Bentley is being such an ass. He was really nice when he was at our house for that short time, and Owen still enjoys working for him."

I shrug. "It was a one-night stand. There's no need to be sorry. I just need him to cooperate long enough to make sure I don't fuck up this fundraiser. The owner of the shelter is my boss's mother. Not sure if I shared that before, but it's really important to me that I don't disappoint her. My boss is who recommended me for my new role at work."

Piper takes a drink and smiles. "How's that going, by the way?"

I grin. "It's demanding of my time, but the challenge these new projects give me is exactly what I needed."

Ella laughs. "You're such a nerd, and I love you so much."

I wrap an arm around her and put my drink between my legs so that I can place my other arm around Piper.

"I love you both so fucking much that it hurts my soul. Never again can we go this long without having a hang out. Even if it's just lunch. If we don't make time, it will pass much too quickly."

Ella and Piper squeeze me hard, and tingles move along my skin. I'm not normally one to get all mushy, but I really don't know what I'd do without them in my life. They're my ride or dies, my Golden Girls, my everything.

When we finally separate, I take a long pull from my wine bottle and get out my phone to turn on some music. When I'm done, my thumb hovers near my messages, but I quickly toss my phone onto the table.

Nope, I have no reason to reach out to Bentley. He's

been sending me what I need via email, and that works for our situation.

Ella stands and pulls me and Piper up with her. "We can't have music without dancing."

With my best friends alongside me, I forget about my phone, Bentley, and everything else but these two incredible women who mean the world to me.

Tonight is for us. Tomorrow, or maybe even never, will be soon enough to sort out my desires for one Bentley Abbott.

Chapter Twelve

A LOT MORE WORK

Bentley

WORK HAS BEEN KICKING MY ASS. THIS COMPANY is an even bigger mess than I realized at first, but the bones are there, and the employees have been agreeable to change. While that makes things easier, it doesn't mean there is less shit to get done.

Between all of my meetings, emails, conference calls, and the fundraiser, I've hardly slept in the last week. We only have six more weeks to get everything lined up, and I haven't done enough for the donations.

I'm sure Joyce will point that out when she asks me for an update during the meeting that's supposed to be starting any minute. Though, currently, I'm sitting in my car, avoiding going in.

I can already see Kenzie's white Honda. I've avoided her as much as possible. Every time I think of that woman, I get angrier with myself for letting things get so damn complicated.

Her fiery personality and hair to match are hard to get out of my head. I don't know why. And the less I want to think about the reasons, the more Kenzie's face appears in my mind.

Her creamy, fair skin. The way her eyes look more green than hazel when she's angry with me. How her auburn hair falls in subtle waves around her face, and how soft it was to grip when I had her in my bed.

My palm slams against the top of the steering wheel. I can't do this. Not right now when I have to face her.

With a huff, I get out of the Range Rover and head inside. Joyce's voice doesn't greet me like normal, so I move the "closed" sign from where it's waiting on the counter to the door, then lock it myself before heading toward the meeting room. As I do, I hear laughter, but when I step inside, the room quiets a little too quickly.

Joyce nods at me but doesn't offer her normal enthusiasm at my arrival. "Looks like we can get started now."

"Good morning to you, too," I say lightly to Joyce when I pass by her and gently squeeze her shoulder.

Her shoulders relax some from the contact.

Kenzie is sitting next to her, and I get stuck between Mary and Charlie.

Joyce holds a paper up to her face and then nods at Sam. "I see you have everything on your list complete. How did budgeting go for all of that?"

He smiles proudly, sitting up straighter and giving a quick glance around the table. "I was able to get half of the materials on donation, so I still have a lot left to work with if you want me to do a few other things."

Joyce tilts her head, and her gaze cuts to me. "Great job, Sam. Maybe you can help Bentley with get going on some of his donations."

When Joyce looks away, I glare at Kenzie. She must have said something to Joyce already, and that's not going to work for me. Kenzie can't keep storming into every aspect of my life and ruining things.

I sit quietly through the rest of the meeting, only answering questions when directly asked and making promises I intend to follow through on, even if it's just so I don't feel like a chastised child when we meet again in two weeks.

Kenzie is the first out of the room when Joyce calls things to an end. I try to go after her so I can have a stern talk with her, but Joyce grabs on to my arm and halts me.

"We need to chat."

Her firm tone leaves no room for argument, and because I respect her so much, I nod and take another seat.

Once everyone else has left, she sits next to me, turning her chair to face me head on. "Have I asked too much of you, Bentley?"

Wrinkles form around her soft eyes, and guilt makes my chest ache at having disappointed one of the few people in this world that I care so much about.

"I don't know what Kenzie told you, but I *am* working on the donations. I've even answered all the questions she's had and given her access to everything I have," I say a little more defensively than I intend.

She shakes her head and grabs my hand on the table. "Kenzie didn't have to tell me anything for me to see what's going on. I know you're not normally this involved, and I appreciate you not telling me no when I first mentioned you taking on a bigger role for this event, but maybe it would have been better if you did."

My brow furrows. "What do you mean?"

She releases her grip on me and leans back in her chair with a sigh. "I have long considered you family, Bentley, so I say this with all the love in my heart, but I don't think you can handle what I've asked of you. At least, not on top of everything else you have going on. I'm going to find another volunteer with event experience this week, and then I'll have you hand over any communications you've already made."

I shake my head, even though this should be a good thing. I didn't want to be more involved, but something about backing out now doesn't sit right with me.

"What if I can get more done this week? Can you give me another chance to try harder?" I ask while my foot bounces under the table.

She tilts her head. "You don't want an out? From your lack of partnership with Kenzie, I assumed you would be jumping for joy at this idea."

"What does that mean?" My voice lowers, and I instantly feel bad for my tone. Joyce isn't the problem here.

She picks at something on her shirt and smiles. "Calm down, Bentley. Kenzie said the same as you. That you did everything she asked, but she didn't ask much from you. I can assume that's because you're being too much of a man, or you're too busy, or maybe it's a little of both. Either way, I've made my own assumptions based on my many years of acquired wisdom."

Joyce hands me a couple of sheets of paper. I take them. Though, I don't know what I'm looking at.

"All of the other partners have met several times. They've worked together by communicating near daily and helping the other when needed. You and Kenzie are the only two who didn't meet to get work done since our last meeting. I have no doubt in my heart that you want to see Resolutions get the donations they need, but maybe I was wrong in asking for more from you than your business sense."

A vice wraps around my chest, squeezing hard. I hate that I've let Joyce down. I want to blame Kenzie for my lack of efforts, but I'm a grown-ass man and I should have done better.

I drum my fingers on the plastic tabletop. "I'm sorry, Joyce. Give me this week to make things right. I'll call Kenzie and set up a meeting with her, so we can get on the same page with the tasks you've asked of us."

She gives her head a slight shake, but says nothing, so I add, "Please, let me make this right."

Our eyes lock, and I don't back down. I should, but I can't. The need to see this through is strong, regardless of how busy I am at work or how much better it would be for me to stay away from Kenzie.

Joyce sighs, and her shoulders drop. "Fine, but you only get this week. If I don't see progress by Monday, then you're done with the fundraiser...besides writing that big check I know you like giving me every year."

Her wrinkled lips lift into a smile, and I stand, pulling Joyce into a hug. "Thank you. I won't let you down again."

Joyce pats my back. "I know. You're a good man,

Bentley. You just need to show more people that side of you. Not just little old ladies like me."

I take a step toward the door. "Hey, my new employees like me just fine."

She nods. "I'm sure they do, but I'm not getting any younger. You might not be blood, but I've enjoyed getting to know your heart over the years. I want to see you happy before I leave this world."

My throat aches. "I am happy."

She tsks. "If you think that, then I've got a lot more work to do with you."

Joyce shuffles past me, and I try not to dwell on her comment. Instead, I head toward the front door, ignoring the meowing cat on the front desk, and pull my phone out of my pocket.

I have a lunch meeting to plan with a woman I probably need to apologize to but really don't want to.

Chapter Thirteen

A CROOKED DICK

Kenzie

WHEN I GET BACK TO WORK FROM THE fundraiser meeting, I head straight to my office. I haven't had any time to hang anything on the walls, but I smile when I see the picture of me, Ella, and Piper next to my computer screen. Our girl's night had been just what we all needed, and I was already itching for another one.

Partly because I could never get enough of my best friends and also because, at the moment, it felt like I couldn't get enough distractions to keep from thinking about Bentley.

Joyce asked so many questions about him when I showed up early for the meeting. I didn't know how to answer half of them, and her inquisitiveness made me believe she was frustrated, but there's no telling if that was because of me or the man in question.

When he finally showed up, I avoided his gaze and got

the hell out of there before he could either pretend that I didn't exist or say something to piss me off.

Now, I'm wondering if that was the right choice. He was polite to me in the emails. Maybe I'm making more of a thing out of this than I should be. We'd had sex. Big deal. It wasn't like it was the first time for either of us.

Except I can't stop thinking about said sex.

I know that's my problem. I don't want to get to know Bentley any more than I have to. I don't want him to reject me again or to know he's actually a nice guy behind his grumpy demeanor.

I just want to move on and find someone who can give me orgasms like he did, but isn't a complete dick.

Once I'm seated at my desk, I dig my phone out of the black hole that is my purse and see I have a text message. Shit. Not from who I expect, either.

Fucker: I wanted to talk to you after the meeting, but Joyce needed to speak with me. Can we meet for lunch this week?

Maybe "Fucker" is a bit dramatic for his contact info, but what can I say? The man hurt my pride.

Me: I can make tomorrow work.

I set my phone down and log into my computer. By the time my email is pulled up, I've glanced at my phone a dozen times to see if he's responded.

Maybe lunch isn't such a good idea. Maybe sticking to email would be better. I don't trust myself not to say something he doesn't need to know if we're alone together.

Me: Never mind. This week doesn't work.

Fucker: I just made reservations at Charlie's for 1pm tomorrow.

Our messages come through at the same time. So, he wasn't ignoring my response, he was reserving a time with the restaurant. Damn it. I don't know if that's better or worse.

Fucker: Don't cancel on me.

Fucker: Please.

For the love of all the dildos in the world. He just said *please*. How am I supposed to ignore that?

I can't. I should, but I can't.

Me: Who are you and what did you do with the asshole?

Fucker: I deserve that. I'll try to be less of an asshole in your presence for lunch.

Joyce must have said something to Bentley. I don't trust this nice guy act, but I am curious. Just enough to make me ignore the potential consequences of said curiosity.

Me: I'll meet you at Charlie's at 1pm tomorrow.

Fucker: Thank you, Kenzie.

My core tightens, and I try not to picture his rigid cock in the shower when I shove my phone across my desk. I have too much work to get done today. I can't think about Bentley anymore. At least, not until tomorrow afternoon.

Damn it. I'm in so much trouble.

———

I HAVE DARK CIRCLES UNDER MY EYES, MY MUSCLES ache, and I want to nap on my lunch break, but instead, I'm headed to meet Bentley for lunch. I worried I'd be nervous, but I'm too fucking exhausted to even care.

Being in charge of certain programs has its benefits, but

last night, when a server crashed, I was the lucky employee to get the call. I ended up being at work until two in the morning, asleep around three, and awake again at six.

I feel like death. I'm not even positive my heels are the same color. One might be navy blue while the other is black. I don't know and don't care.

My stomach rumbles when I pull into my parking spot just a few cars down from Bentley's black Range Rover. I could get down with his heated leather seats right about now.

I lean my head forward on the steering wheel and close my eyes for just a moment to ease the burning inside them. Then, I nearly jump out of my seat when someone knocks on my window.

Bentley is bending down and staring at me with a raised brow.

Shit. Did I fall asleep?

One glance at the clock in my car says yes, but only for a few minutes. It's five after one, so I'm not terribly late.

I unbuckle and grab my purse before opening my door. In my haste, I don't realize that Bentley is still standing there, and the handle hits his right hip.

"Fuck, Kenzie," he growls.

I finish getting out and quickly shut my door. "I'm sorry. I didn't mean to. It's just been—"

"Doubtful," he says, cutting me off.

I shove at his chest, and he stumbles into my car. "Listen here, asshole. I've had one hell of a night and day. I don't need any shit from you. Not today."

He raises a brow. "Late night at the bar again?"

"Fuck. You."

I reach for my door again and barely have it open when he pushes it back closed.

I'm so angry and tired and overwhelmed that my eyes fill with tears that I don't want. Not now, and especially not in front of this man.

He reaches for me, but I flinch back.

"I'm sorry, Kenzie. I thought you were standing me up, and I got angry. I didn't realize you'd had a bad day."

I glance up at him, wanting to stay pissed, but his swirling blue eyes capture me, and a bit of the tension leaves my body.

"I'm hungry," I say.

He steps to the side and gestures toward the restaurant. "Then, let's go inside."

He doesn't smile, doesn't touch me, doesn't do anything other than wait for me to make my choice.

I should leave, but I smell pasta and bread, and I need sustenance badly. And caffeine.

Fuck. I might as well stay and make him pay for my meal.

I lock my car and move ahead of him. When we get to the front of the brick building, he reaches for the wooden door and holds it open for me.

A "thank you" sits on the tip of my tongue, but instead, I stay silent. He hasn't earned niceties from me yet.

A host in a white collared dress shirt and black bowtie stares at Bentley. "Mr. Abbott, I thought you'd left."

"Yes, seems there was a misunderstanding. Is my table still available?" Bentley asks respectfully.

The young man nods. "Of course, sir. I'll have some new waters brought out for you and your guest."

Bentley nods and presses his hand lightly over my lower back. I stiffen from his touch and wish he would have just led the way by walking in front of me.

Instead, we stay side by side until we're at a table for two near the back. It's quiet and dim and private. I don't like it.

Plus, I know I'm a wreck and feel like everyone is staring at me. I barely brushed my hair, and there are wrinkles in my dress pants that I hate. Hopefully, my makeup is at least still where it should be.

Bentley waits until I sit before taking his seat, then a server arrives with two waters. A lemon rests on top of the ice, and I pick it out before the tangy taste can taint my drink.

The server raises a brow at me but says nothing as she tucks a strand of loose blonde hair behind her ear and sets the menus down. "I'll be back in a few to get your order."

She disappears, but not before giving Bentley a once-over.

I keep quiet and place my lemon on the white tablecloth, uncaring if it's not the right thing to do in the fancy restaurant. I've heard of this place before and thought it was just a nice Italian eatery, but apparently, there's a reason I've never been here prior to today.

I don't really fit in.

Without looking at Bentley again, I grab the menu and glance over the options. I spot lobster and grin at the one-hundred-dollar price tag, but when my stomach grumbles again, I go for something I know I'll enjoy: chicken alfredo with a side salad and bread.

When I set the menu down, Bentley is staring at me.

"What?" I ask.

His jaw tightens and eyes narrow while he looks me over. "What happened?"

I give my head a small shake, ignoring the warmth simmering in my core. "Don't insult me by asking a question that you don't care about the answer to. I don't know why you wanted this lunch, but I know it's not to catch up about our lives."

He leans forward. "You think you know me so well?"

My eyes roam over him. "I know enough."

The server returns, setting a basket of bread in the middle of the small table, then angles her body toward Bentley. "Have we decided what we want?"

Her voice is sweet, but he's still staring at me. "Ladies first."

Reluctantly, the server turns toward me. I keep my eyes locked on Bentley for a second longer, then address the server. "I'll take the chicken alfredo and a side salad with no onions, please."

She nods and writes down a few notes before Bentley gives his order.

"I'll have the alfredo but with shrimp. Oh, and I'll take extra onions on my salad." He reaches across the table and takes my menu before handing them both to the server, still without looking away from me.

She sighs softly. "I'll have the salads out in just a few."

When she leaves, I chuckle. "I'm not eating my salad, thanks to you."

His head cocks. "What did I do?"

I nod toward where the server disappeared to. "You

ignored her. She's going to be annoyed by that, but she won't take it out on you. No, she'll mess with my food."

"Then, you can have mine," he says easily.

My lips thin. "No way. Not when you asked for extra onions. That's the devil's food right there."

Bentley laughs. The sound is deep and makes my chest vibrate.

"That's a bit dramatic. I'm sure your salad will be fine," he says.

I play with the end of my butter knife. "Why did you invite me here?"

He adjusts his tie and meets my curious gaze. "Because we need to learn to work together, and we didn't start off great. I'm hoping we can come to a mutual understanding and find common ground, like doing whatever it takes to help Resolutions."

I want to chuckle, but instead, I show my amusement with words. "So, you regret kicking me out of your bed after fucking me?"

The server shows back up with salads and promptly drops them on the table without saying a word. I guess I should have looked around before speaking. Though, I'm not embarrassed, and, at this point, I don't really care if Bentley is.

Bentley glowers at me. "Was it really necessary to say that out loud?"

"Is it really necessary to shove that stick up your ass every day?" I retort with a sweet smile.

He picks up a fork and stabs at his food. "As necessary as these extra onions." He shovels the disgusting vegetable into his mouth.

I shudder. "You're repulsive."

"Says the pot to the kettle." His food crunches loudly, and I want to punch him in the face.

Instead of eating my salad, I finally grab a piece of bread and take a massive bite, because why not. The garlic explodes in my mouth, and I moan without thinking. "God, that's so good."

Something thuds against the table. I glance at Bentley to find his darkening eyes on me, the fork upside down on the tablecloth, and his salad long forgotten.

I pick up the bread bowl. "Want one?"

He shakes his head, picks up the dropped utensil, and pays attention to his food again.

After I finish my slice of perfection, I return to our conversation. "So, you want to actually work together on this fundraiser? Why now?"

Bentley chews slowly and wipes a napkin over his perfect lips before speaking. "Because I care about the shelter and Joyce. I want to see things go better than planned."

I tilt my head. "So, Joyce said something to you and now you're backpedaling."

His attitude changed too fast for there to be any other reason for this impromptu lunch.

"Joyce might have spoken with me yesterday, but I was already wanting to figure out a solution before she said anything. I'd like to see what you've gotten done and what I need to help with still."

He pauses when the host arrives with our food. "Your server is on break. I hope everything is to your liking."

I smile at the young man. "Thank you. It looks amazing."

He nods and leaves without another word.

I swirl pasta around my fork and look back up at Bentley. "Listen, this is just as frustrating for me as it is for you."

He snorts while moving his chair closer to the table. "Doubtful."

I cut a glare at him for interrupting me. "*But* I'm willing to put past encounters behind us if you apologize for being a prick to me that first night."

Bentley pauses with his fork in the air. "Excuse me?"

I take my bite, slowly chewing and swallowing before I answer. "You heard me."

"Why?" he demands.

"Why should you apologize? If you need to ask that, you have bigger problems than me being a pain in your ass."

He takes another bite of pasta and stares intently at his food. His knuckles are white from holding his fork so tightly.

"Fine."

"Fine? That's a swell apology," I deadpan.

Bentley looks me straight in the eyes and leans forward. I can't help but mimic his actions. The table suddenly feels too small. He puts both of his hands on the table and says, "I'm sorry, Kenzie. I shouldn't have brought you home the other night."

Oh, that fucking dickass.

It takes every ounce of self-control that I possess not to throw my water in his face.

"And I'm sorry you were born with a crooked dick." I

move my chair back and grab my bag. "Don't bother to invite me to another lunch. I won't accept."

I walk from the table and head for the front door. Cool air from outside soothes my heated face as I storm away from the building. When I make it to the parking lot, I want to scream. Hell, I want to key his SUV like a damned teenager.

Instead, I unlock my car and get in like the responsible adult I am. As soon as I pop the door open, I hear my name, but that doesn't stop me. Once I'm in my seat, I close the door and hit the lock button.

Fuck Bentley and his talented, not-actually-crooked dick. I don't want anything to do with him.

When I start my car, he pulls on the handle. I hold my middle finger up to the window and put the car in reverse.

"If you back out, you're going to run over my foot," he calls through the window.

"And I'll wish it was your head, so I never have to see your face again." I inch the car back. "Move, Bentley."

He lowers himself so we can see each other. "No. We need to work together."

I scoff. "You should have thought about that before being such a dick."

One of his hands slams against the window, getting my full attention. "I'm sorry, Kenzie."

I glare at him and back up a little further. "For what?"

He sighs. "You're really going to make me do this?"

I smile. "Abso-fucking-lutely."

He shifts and settles himself onto one knee. I don't know if the move is purposeful or just because he's tired of crouching, but I like seeing him on this lower level.

My foot stays on the brake, and I meet his heated eyes while he speaks through the window. "I'm sorry for treating you with disrespect at my house. I'm sorry for being angry that you showed up at Resolutions. I'm sorry for not helping you these past two weeks and for acting like a child."

My fingers drum over the steering wheel. I wanted to hate his apology, but it wasn't terrible. In fact, I kind of liked it.

Still, he needs to pay a little more.

I begin to roll the window down and smile. He relaxes and leans back on his feet, just far enough away that I can keep reversing the car.

"Goodbye, Bentley," I say, then back out of the space and put my window back up as I go.

"You've got to be fucking kidding me?" he snarls.

I put the car in drive and grin widely as I wave goodbye.

Let him stew on that for a bit.

Chapter Fourteen

A SEXY FUCKING DISASTER

Bentley

KENZIE CHASE HAS TO BE THE MOST INFURIATING woman I've ever known. I can't believe she just left after my apology. Sure, I'd been more of a dick to her than I intended, but damn it, she brings out the worst in me.

Thanks to her stunt at the restaurant, I accomplished nearly nothing at work. Now I'm at home, trying to salvage the day after having spent an hour in my gym, taking out my aggressions.

Just as I power up my computer, the doorbell echoes through the house. I ignore it, knowing my sister would have let herself in and I don't have time for anyone else.

I log into the company's secure server and pull up my email, then the bell rings again.

"Go the fuck away," I mutter.

As I click on a few things, the bell rings a third, fourth, and fifth time. All consecutive and each more annoying than the prior chimes.

I shove away from my desk and head to the front door without thinking about anything other than pummeling whoever is incessantly hitting that damn button.

My fingers jerk the lock back, and I yank open the door. "What?" I snap before noticing who is on the other side.

Kenzie's hazel eyes widen and roam over my bare chest before dropping to inspect my gray sweatpants a little too closely, given how we parted ways earlier.

She licks her lips, and a sound leaves her throat that has my dick awakening.

When her eyes finally meet mine, they're full of heat, and I can't control my actions.

I reach for her hand and pull her inside the house. Once the door is shut, I push her against it. Her chest rises and falls rapidly, and she presses closer to me while looking up into my penetrating gaze.

My palms flatten against the wood surface and only our hips are touching. I catch her hands flexing in my peripherals.

"What are you doing here, Kenzie?" I ask, my voice rough with the restraint it's taking not to touch her any more than I already am.

Her tongue darts out again, and she pushes closer. "I have no fucking clue."

"Then, let me help you figure it out," I say right before my lips capture hers.

The right thing to do, after the way she took off earlier, would be to get her all worked up and kick her out again. Well, maybe not right, but it would make me feel better.

At least, that's what I think until she reaches for my cock with one hand and the other grips my neck as she pulls out of the kiss. "If you have any intentions of kicking me out, you better do it now, Bentley Abbott."

Fuck, I should. This woman shouldn't even be in my house, let alone ready to let me fuck her senseless again.

Except I can't find it within me to push her away this time.

I enjoy the way she challenges me and, even if it might be the death of me, I'm not kicking her out. Not tonight.

My arms wrap around her, and I lift her into my arms. "You're not going anywhere other than my bed, Kenzie Chase."

"You better hurry before I change my mind." Her fingers tangle into my hair, and she jerks my mouth back to hers.

I shake my head slightly as she does. She's insufferable, but so damn irresistible.

This is a disaster in the making, I think as I carry her up the stairs to my bedroom.

A sexy fucking disaster.

When we enter my room, I toss Kenzie onto my bed and flip her over. I don't want to see the smirk on her face. Not when we both know I was the one who wanted to keep space between us. Yet, here I am, groping her ass and tugging her jeans from her hips.

Kenzie helps with her pants, and when her ass is on display for me, I palm one of the cheeks before raising my hand and quickly lowering it.

The smack echoes through the room, followed by Kenzie's moan. She lowers her head to the bed, and her ass presses closer to me.

I leave her there and grab a condom from the nightstand.

In the seconds it takes me to discard my sweatpants, put the condom on, and return, she's turned over. Her shirt and bra are missing, and her legs are spread open for me.

Her pussy is still smooth, without the slightest bit of stubble showing, making me believe that she's a fan of waxing. Suddenly, so am I. My eyes travel up her stomach, over her perfect tits, and find her gaze on my cock.

There's no smirk on her face when she reaches for me. "Fuck me, Bentley."

I intend to do that and so much more.

My fingers move over her breasts and further down until they find her clit and slip inside her tight pussy.

She pushes down on my hand and moans. "Not like that."

I know what this vixen wants. The me from that first night would have made her wait, but fuck. I'd be lying if I said I didn't want the same thing: my dick driving hard into her slick heat.

I nudge her further onto the mattress and move between her legs. Once I'm situated on my knees, I don't give Kenzie any warning before I lift her hips and thrust inside her ready and waiting pussy.

Her arms spread out, and her nails dig into my pillows while she cries out, muttering, "Fuck, yes."

I lean forward and lower myself before placing my hand on her stomach, positioning her right where I want before I continue fucking her into oblivion.

Kenzie's hips match my movements, and our rhythm is perfectly in sync. She eagerly takes everything I have to offer, and I don't have to worry about being careful with this woman. She's strong and fierce and knows exactly what she wants.

"Oh, God. I'm so close." One of her hand's moves between her legs and I'm reminded of her first night here when she touched herself in my shower.

Hot as that might be, I can't let her push her own orgasm over the edge.

That's my fucking job.

I pause my thrusts and growl out my words. "Hands stay on the pillows."

She whimpers but does as I say and is rewarded when I fuck her harder and faster than before. My fingers trail around her hips, following the dips that lead to her pussy until I find her clit.

When I press against the sweet spot, Kenzie's head rears back and ass lifts higher off the bed to meet my movements. "Don't fucking stop."

Sweat builds on the back of my neck from the increased pace, and my muscles ache, but I'm not even close to done with this woman.

She tightens around me, and I fight to hold back my own release. Her body shudders, and goosebumps rise along her exposed skin.

Her head hangs forward, and I stay buried inside her until she begins to move again.

"More?" I ask.

"Always more," she answers, voice rough.

I pull out of her and lay on the bed. "Good answer. Now, fuck me like you hate me."

She smirks. "Not a problem."

Kenzie climbs on top of me, and her nails bite into my skin, somehow making my dick even harder than before.

I know I should end this. I know I shouldn't have even let her into my house, let alone my bed for a second time, but as she rides me hard and dirty, I can't find the will to push her away.

This time, I'll let Kenzie sleep in my bed, and tomorrow will have to be soon enough to figure out what to do next with this wild woman who has blown into my world like a damn tornado.

Chapter Fifteen

FIGHTING AND FUCKING

Kenzie

I'D GONE TO BENTLEY'S HOUSE TO TELL HIM I WAS done playing games and that I would accept his apology if it was still on the table. Then, he'd answered the door half naked, and the only thought I could focus on was how his gray sweatpants left *nothing* to the imagination.

Before I knew it, we were in his bedroom and fucking the sense right out of each other. I rode the shit out of him, taking out any lingering aggressions while I marked his chest with my nails. When he finally came, I'm pretty sure he lost consciousness for a moment, thanks to my talented hips, and I fell into a heap on his soft mattress.

Even though Bentley said he wouldn't kick me out, I decide to leave on my own this time. It's nearing one in the morning, and I'm going to be exhausted again tomorrow. Though, the ache between my legs reminds me that fucking Bentley is well worth any loss of sleep.

I get in my car and look back up at his monstrous

house. That man is more of a contradiction than anything else I've ever encountered.

Before I can change my mind, I put the car in drive and head home to my studio apartment where there is little-to-no privacy in the space outside of the small bathroom.

I reach to turn the radio on and drown out thoughts of Bentley, but not even the hip-hop music blasting through my car can make me ignore the growing feelings I have for that pain-in-the-ass man.

I've always heard that the line between love and hate was blurry, but I never understood the saying until now. Not that I'm even close to falling in love with Bentley Abbott, but I can see myself fighting and fucking him for the foreseeable future, toeing that line just to see which side I end up on.

Just depends on how he reacts to being left.

I'm not usually one to play games, but something about Bentley drives me to the brink of insanity and makes me do things I normally wouldn't.

Within twenty minutes, I'm home, stripped naked, and the scent of Bentley's woodsy cologne still clings to me. I take a deep inhale and close my eyes.

Tomorrow will be an interesting day.

———

When I wake to my alarm, I stretch and groan. My sore muscles remind me of the night before, and I let out a sigh of happiness. When I reach for my phone to turn off the beeping, there's a text on my screen.

Fucker: You left.

They're only two words, but they sure do make me grin.

Me: I did.

I get in the shower and ready for work before I check my phone again. I tap the screen and there are no new notifications.

Well, okay, then. Off to work I go.

I check the weather and decide it's still warm enough out for a dress that I can pair with my new tan boots. The flower print hangs loosely around my waist and hits my knees, so it's still modest enough for work, especially with the capped shoulders.

Once I'm dressed, I head to the office and forget about my phone for more than half the day. There are meetings to lead, employees to update, assignments to follow up on, and codes to fix.

As much as I'd like to know if Bentley cares that I left, I just don't have the time.

When I do find a free moment, it's nearing two in the afternoon. There's a thread of texts from Piper and Ella in our group chat that I'll have to get to later and one from Bentley, sent just after I got to work.

Fucker: Why?

I should probably change his name to something more appropriate, but I focus more on the singular question. He at least cares enough to wonder why I didn't wait until the morning to leave as he must have expected.

Me: Because I'm a grown woman and wanted to go home. Is that a problem?

I browse the texts from my best friends. Poor Piper still has no idea how to solve her work problems, and I feel for her. Maybe this is a sign that she shouldn't abandon us for California. Though, I'll never tell her that. I might be selfish at times, but not when it comes to Ella and Piper. They get the best of me.

Fucker: Not a problem. Just surprised.

Me: Any regrets?

The typing icon pops up and goes away several times before he finally responds.

Fucker: No.

Simple and to the point. I like it.

Me: Good.

I put my phone away again and scarf down the sandwich that was delivered two hours ago, then get my ass back to work.

———

THAT NIGHT, I GET HOME LATE AND EAT A BOWL of cereal for dinner, because why not. After a quick shower, I'm changed into my silk pajama shorts and a cami before settling in on the couch.

I'm two seconds from starting a video group chat with my girls when I get a text message from Bentley.

Fucker: We need to work on the fundraiser.

I smirk, wondering if that's all he wants to work on.

Me: Where and when?

Fucker: Your house, now.

I jump off the couch and head to the east window that overlooks the parking lot. My fingers part the blinds, and I peek down.

Shit. I spot Bentley's Range Rover idling in one of the

visitor spaces. I don't know how he figured out where I live, but I'm not prepared for guests.

I go back to grab my phone and tell him I'm not home, but there's another text waiting on my screen when I get back to the couch.

Fucker: On my way up.

Double shit. He's not going to let me keep him out.

Instead of bothering to open my phone and reply, I hurry to my kitchen and make as many dirty dishes disappear as possible. Including my not-quite-finished cereal bowl that ends up in the fridge, along with some cups I don't want to confuse with clean ones later in the cabinets.

Next, I tackle my clothes. Thankfully, those are easier to hide. I toss every clothing item I see into the laundry basket even if I don't think it's dirty. I'm realizing now I should maybe pick up my shit more often, but in my defense, it's been a long-ass week and I haven't had the energy to do any adulting.

Especially since I wasn't expecting guests.

There's a knock on my door, and my stomach flutters.

I take a deep breath, smooth my hands over my sides, and gasp. "I'm wearing pajamas," I mutter in horror.

He's seen me naked, but still. I should probably put more clothes on before he thinks I don't want to work on the fundraiser, because I really do.

"Open the door, Kenzie," he demands.

Fuck it. He asked for this.

My feet carry me across the room, and I unlock the deadbolt, then release the chain. When I swing the door open, his chest rumbles.

"Where are your clothes?" he asks.

I shrug. "I had a long day, and this is what I wear at home when I'm not prepared for visitors."

His chest rises and falls slowly before he finally takes a step forward.

I move out of his way and shut the door behind him. "This is just temporary. I'm looking to buy a place soon."

Suddenly, I'm self-conscious of my meager lifestyle. Then, I give myself a mental bitch slap. Absolutely not. I won't be ashamed of supporting myself. Bentley can fuck himself if he thinks less of me just because I don't live in a mansion.

He looks around and nods. "I'd rather have this than my place. Less space to lose shit in."

My thighs tighten at his acceptance. I didn't expect that.

Bentley takes a seat on my couch and stretches out. His wide form takes up half of the space, and I'm not sure how I feel about seeing him there so comfortable.

He's wearing jeans and a dark-blue polo that makes his icy eyes stand out. His hair lays flat, making me assume he either didn't style it today or he's already showered since getting off work.

His gaze finds mine. "Are you going to sit?"

"Let me just grab my laptop." I head for my nightstand where I left it and unplug the charging cord.

I spot my robe and consider covering up since we're supposed to be working, but Bentley seems capable of remaining on task, so I ignore the black material hanging on the wall.

When I sit down, I set the laptop on the coffee table and pull it closer to the couch. A few clicks later and I have the saved spreadsheet pulled up. It's color-coded and geeked out, but it works for me.

Bentley chuckles, and I look over at him. "What?"

He shakes his head. "Absolutely nothing. Where should we start?"

My phone vibrates, but I don't see it on the couch. Bentley raises up and grabs it from under his ass. His eyes glance at the screen as he hands me the phone. His brow lifts. "Fucker? Really?"

I ignore his question and see a message from our group chat.

Piper: I got the move date today. It's locked in this time. Even if the new building isn't done, they'll have space for me at the current site. December 27th.

My heart sinks. It doesn't matter that I've had months to prepare for this moment or that there are still months left until she goes. It's still not easy to accept that one of my best friends is going to be moving all the way across the country from me.

Sure, it will be nice to leave North Carolina and visit California, but how often will I get to do that? Not as much as I'd like. I know that for sure.

Ella: Congrats, Pipe! We'll celebrate soon. I'm so happy for you!

I quickly type out a response before I get too pouty.

Me: About fucking time! Can't wait to plan your party. Would strippers be too much?

Piper: Don't you dare.

I laugh, because they know I would.

"I thought something was wrong, but you're laughing," Bentley says, staring at me more intently than I expect.

I set the phone down on the coffee table. "My best friend is moving to California by the end of the year."

Bentley's eyes widen. "Owen is leaving?"

"Not Ella. Piper. She's the responsible one out of the three of us. Not sure what will happen once she's not here to police things." I smirk, thinking of all the times Piper has kept me from going home with a guy I shouldn't have or prevented me from doing something that I could end up in jail for. Misdemeanors only, of course, but still. She balances out my crazy in a way nobody ever could.

Bentley sits forward, his expression softening. "If you're not up for working now, we can meet again tomorrow."

I grab my laptop and put it on my thighs. "No, I'm good. There's nothing I can do right now about her moving, so might as well keep my mind busy."

He settles back on the couch, still surprising me with how at ease he is in my home. "Are you going to change my name in your phone?"

I chuckle. "Why? Does it offend you?"

"It's childish," he deadpans, looking me straight in the eyes.

I tilt my head forward. "Growing up is for losers. I intend to be a child my whole life. It's better than having a stick up my ass."

His lips thin, and I turn my gaze back to the laptop before I continue to speak. "So, Joyce wanted us to get rental items reserved, donations secured to not only pay for all of these things, but hold the shelter over for at least six months of expenses, and also lock in some sort of food for the event."

I point to the screen and go on. "Each task has its own

tab. After reviewing the past events and thinking I was going to be doing this on my own, I started with how to feed the masses and chose food trucks. There is plenty of room for three of them. I have a taco truck and one that does burgers and hotdogs already reserved for the day. I hadn't decided what would be good for the third."

When I glance at Bentley, he's taking in all the information on the screen, and he's moved closer. Our thighs are touching, and the heat from his skin is seeping through his jeans and straight to my core.

"We should do a beverage truck. Preferably one that will donate a portion of the profits to the shelter and serves beer. That will be helpful for the evening crowd. I actually might know a guy." He pulls out his phone and starts typing. "I'll take care of that since you already handled the other two."

Well, that was easy.

I click on the next tab for rental items. This one is more complicated, but I understand my crazy. So, I start to explain my columns and the boxes next to them. Except when I'm only halfway through, Bentley takes the laptop from me.

"Hey, that's rude," I say with a slight pout.

He rolls his eyes. "I'm not an invalid. You don't have to dumb everything down for me. Let me just take a look, and I can ask questions when I have them if that works for you."

Okay, maybe he has a point there.

I lean back onto the couch cushion. "Just don't change anything or I'll kill you."

He snorts but keeps his eyes on the screen.

My eyes watch his fingers like a hawk. I worked hard on

organizing all that information, and I'll be damned if I let him screw it up.

Too many minutes later, he finally hands my laptop back. "I like what you did with the booth items and bigger things like the dunk tank and ponies. Do the green ones mean donated?"

I nod. "I contacted as many people as I could who the shelter had done business with in the past and hoped repeat business would help. Orange means they at least discounted the service fee and red is full price. I figured that would help for planning other events as well, depending on what's needed in the future."

His palms smooth over his jeans. "Very smart of you. Have you asked for any monetary donations?"

I raise a brow at him, fighting a smile. "Isn't that your job?"

He grins. "I said I'd handle that, and I will. I was just wondering if you'd taken it upon yourself to show me up."

One of my hands runs through my hair as I laugh. "I think all of the tasks I've accomplished do that well enough."

"Fair enough. So that I don't ruin your spreadsheet, I can email you the donation information and you can plug it in here however you see fit?" He points to the laptop.

"That works for me. Do you have any lined up yet?" I ask, my fingers hovering over the keyboard.

His lips downturn. "Just one, but I'll get more this week. Our goal is still fifty thousand, right?"

"Yep. Joyce is hoping for more than half of that up front from business donations if possible and the rest to be made the day of the event," I answer, then ask, "Who is the one donor you have already?"

Our gazes meet, and heat travels down my chest, straight to my pussy. I try to break the stare, but I can't. Bentley has me captured, and tingles rise along my skin.

He grabs my laptop and sets it carefully on the coffee table. "I think we've covered enough for tonight."

My chest is heaving when I nod.

I'm not sure if Bentley came over here only to work, and if so, I'm going to be sorely disappointed.

He leans over me, and my back sinks further into the couch. "Kenzie."

"Bentley," I say, my voice breathy.

His lips brush over mine. "I should go."

"Or you could stay a little longer," I counter.

He runs his fingers over my collarbone. "It would be a lot longer than a little."

I shudder from the featherlight touch. "I'm okay with that. Sleep is overrated."

My hands reach for his arms, and I tug him closer until he's practically laying on top of me. He really needs to be wearing less clothes.

Just when I get the top button of his jeans undone, his pocket vibrates.

He groans and sits up.

"You're seriously going to answer that?" I huff.

Bentley ignores me, then pulls his phone out. "Shit. I need to go."

He stands and fixes his pants before staring at me still spread out on the couch. "I'd rather be fucking you senseless if that helps soothe your ego."

I grin. "A little. Think of me when you jerk off later. Alone."

His stare darts to my dresser. "Think of me when you settle for less."

I glance back and spot my box of toys sitting on display. Oops. I missed those in my quick clean-up. Whatever. I have no shame.

By the time I turn around again, Bentley is closing the door behind him. I throw my head back on the couch, not even remotely interested in settling for less than the off-the-charts orgasms I know he's capable of giving me.

Damn it. How did I let this happen?

Chapter Sixteen

STRICTLY BUSINESS

Bentley

I'D THOUGHT IT WAS A TERRIBLE IDEA TO SHOW UP at Kenzie's apartment after getting her address from Joyce. Even though I knew it wasn't good, I still went there. Her place was exactly what I pictured for her.

Small, but packed full of crazy.

I would have fucked her on every surface of that studio if my sister hadn't texted. Now, instead of making Kenzie scream loud enough for the neighbors to complain, I'm headed toward Celia's bakery.

I don't know what's broken, but she sent a 911 text and those don't get ignored. Not for my baby sister.

Her bakery is downtown and called "Sweet Delights". She got her Associates degree in business and used her trust fund from our grandparents to open this spot two years ago. Our parents thought it was a joke, but now that she's making over a million a year, they're trying to get her to franchise.

Thankfully, Celia knows better than to let them get a hold of her business. Sure, one day she might expand, but for now, she's young and enjoying what she's doing. I'm damned proud of her. Well, as long as I don't have to hear about her dick cookies that she sells online.

When I pull up, I do a once-over of the building. The white paint is pristine, and the windows are painted with colorful cupcakes and cookies. The light-pink door draws the eye, but not annoyingly so.

I get out of my SUV and head inside. The checkered floors are my least favorite, but small white tables cover most of them. The glass shields on the counter sparkle under the dim lights, and I call out for my sister.

"Back here," she yells in return.

Once I'm behind the counter, I smell something burning and quicken my pace, hoping she'd have been smart enough to call the fire department if something was on fire.

There is still smoke in the air, and she's waving a towel around frantically with tears on her cheeks. Her sad blue eyes land on me, and her shoulders drop. "I don't know what happened."

I close the distance between us and wrap my arms around her, uncaring that flour is getting all over me. "It's okay, sis. Tell me what's broken and I'll fix it."

She points to the oven. "I had cookies in there for five minutes. The oven wasn't getting hot enough, so I turned it up. A minute later, there's smoke filling the room and my cookies are crispy instead of moist."

I'm not a mechanic, but I've always had a knack for

following a problem to its source. I might be able to fix her problems tonight if it's what I think it is, but worst case, I'll at least save her some money when she hires a proper repair person if I can narrow some things down.

My thumbs wipe away her tears. "Why are you baking this late anyway?"

She blushes, and I hold up my hands. "Never mind. I don't want to know."

Celia laughs, and I at least feel better that she's cheering up, even if it's at my own expense.

As I start to move the commercial range away from the wall so I can get a look at the wiring, Celia takes a seat on a stool and twiddles her thumbs. "What were you doing? You got here quicker than I expected."

"I was out," I answer, then grunt when the oven gets stuck on a divot in the flooring.

Celia hums. "Out where?"

"Busy here, sis." I shove hard and finally have enough room to get around to the backside.

"Right, but I've seen you multitask before. Your failure to answer tells me it's somewhere I should know about. Did you meet someone?" she asks, talking quickly.

I roll my eyes. "Why does everything always have to do with a woman when I don't want to talk about it?"

She hops off the stool and leans against the oven. "Because I know you, Bentley. The only thing you're private with is your love life, or lack thereof. Who is she?"

I look up to find her hovering over me with a grin on her face. "It's nobody. I was working on fundraiser stuff. Speaking of, you can repay me for tonight by volunteering the day of and working one of the booths. It's carnival-themed."

She claps her hands. "I could do face painting for the kids. My decorating skills come in handy for that."

"That would actually be really great. I'll tell Joyce about it tomorrow," I say after I've unplugged the oven's power source.

There's a fuse that looks blown, and I'm pretty sure the toolkit I bought Celia when she opened has some extras in it.

"Where's that black box I gave you?" I ask her.

She bites her lip. "Um, I think it's in the storage room. Let me go check."

Celia runs off, and I lean against the wall while I wait for her.

When I close my eyes, I picture Kenzie's hard nipples that I could see through her silk pajama top. I give my head a solid shake. I can't have those thoughts right now. Not when I'm supposed to be helping my sister.

She returns several minutes later, huffing. "Found it. Under the register."

I raise a brow and take it from her. "Probably not the best place for it."

She shrugs. "I've had to increase my flour orders, and I'm running out of space to keep up with all of these dic—special cookies and now people want waffles, but I don't think I can ship those and keep them fresh without increasing pricing too much. Though, I'm thinking of commissioning some molds that I can sell. Something where another company makes and ships them for me and takes a small profit. I could still make money and not do all the work, you know?"

I dig through the box and find the fuse I need. "That's a great idea. You've made yourself a brand, and you should capitalize on that. Merchandising can be huge if you do it right. Do you have a marketing person to help you?"

Celia is all smiles. "I do. I just hired him in fact, so I'm glad you agree about merchandise stuff, because that's what he recommended, too."

I give her my full attention. "Hired *him*? Who is he?"

She shoves me. "Oh, calm down, big brother. You can have his name if he actually asks me out. Right now, I'm keeping things strictly business until I see how he performs."

Oh, God. That word makes my mind go places it shouldn't, so I can't continue the conversation.

"Make sure he knows you have a brother who will murder him if he disrespects you." I go back to fixing the oven, hoping this one fuse will solve Celia's problems for the night.

Once I'm done, I straighten the mess of wires, plug the cord back into the wall, and push the oven back to where it was. "Try it now."

I head to the shelves where I spot fudge brownies and grab a package as payment for my help. I open the box and eat one while we wait for the oven to hopefully heat properly this time.

Within five minutes, it's up to temp and Celia is jumping up and down. Her arms wrap around my waist. "Thank you so much. I don't know what I'd do without you."

I hug her back just as tightly. "Always here for you, Ce."

She pulls back, but holds my hands before I can walk away. "I hope you're happy, Bentley. You deserve that."

Before I can respond to her, the front door opens and a shrill voice I recognize echoes through the shop. "Celia, honey. Where are you? Are you okay?"

Selene saunters in, flicking her perfectly straight ebony hair behind her shoulders, and wearing a worried expression that turns to feigned shock when she sees me.

"Bentley? I didn't know you were coming to the rescue. The phone cut out before I heard what our Celia was going to do about her little baking problem."

I glance at my sister, who shrugs. "I was on the phone with her when the smoke started."

With a sigh, I step toward the door. "Well, everything's fixed, so I'm leaving."

Selene captures my hand and juts her lower lip out. "But I just got here."

"And you're welcome to stay." I jerk my hand back and nod at my sister. "Let me know if you need anything else."

She waves, and I make a swift retreat. I'm at my car door when I see Selene chasing after me in her obnoxious heels that click loudly on the concrete.

"Come on, Bentley. Just talk to me for a minute. After all we've been through, I deserve that, don't I?" She waits on the sidewalk while I stew over her words.

I want to be a dick, but she knows just what to say to make me give pause, something I should have seen as a red flag over a year ago.

"About what? I thought we'd said what we'd needed to

when you called before," I reply, still holding on to my door handle.

She comes closer, running her fingers over my hood before she gets within a few feet of me. She puts weight on her left foot, and her right hip pops out while she leans against the Range Rover.

"I miss you. After everything we've been through, I feel like we owe it to ourselves to give things another chance. I was under pressure from my parents, and I acted out. I didn't mean the things I said before."

I almost ask what "pressure" she's talking about, but I know she's just trying to trap me with her words.

"I'm sorry, Selene. That doesn't change anything for me," I say with as much kindness as I can muster for her.

Her chin shakes and eyes water. "I thought you'd understand. My parents—"

I cut her off. "Can't always be an excuse to do whatever you want. You've had plenty of chances to cut them off from influencing you, and I'm done pretending that you'll change. We're done. Please don't make this any harder than it needs to be. For Celia's sake."

I use my sister in hopes it will make Selene see reason, because for some reason Celia cares about this crazy woman. I'm not sure my tactics will work, and I hope Celia doesn't get hurt in the process.

Selene steps closer. Her palm rests against my chest, and she flutters her eyes at me. "But we're so good together."

Gently, I remove her hand and step back. "We're not getting back together. Not again."

A feeling of satisfaction rises within me that I'm able to withstand her usual tactics. There was a time that her twisted words, bright amber eyes, and soft skin would convince me to do a lot of things I didn't want to, but not anymore.

There isn't a single part of me interested in Selene any longer. Hell, I can't even remember why I fell for her in the first place.

Her smile falls away, and her eyes darken. "Did you meet someone else?"

I could tell her yes, but I don't think that would help, so I avoid answering the question altogether.

"Listen, Selene. We want different things out of life. I'm sure there's someone else out there for you who will come along any day now. You have to move on."

She sniffles. "But I don't want anyone else. I just want you."

I open my SUV. "I'm sorry, but that's not going to happen and it's unfair to you if I pretend otherwise."

I slide into my seat and close the door. By the time I look out the windshield to see if Selene is still standing there, the fake tears are gone, and her face is like a sheet of ice.

Her lips move, and I swear she says, "We'll see about that."

My shoulders shudder as she turns to head back into the bakery. My phone vibrates, and I see a message from my sister.

Celia: I'm sorry. I swear I didn't invite her over.
Me: It's okay. I dealt with her.

Hopefully, I think and hurriedly put the car into drive, so I can leave before Selene tries anything else.

I head back to Providence, even though my hands itch to turn the wheel back to Kenzie's place downtown.

She could make me forget about seeing Selene again, but that probably wouldn't be right of me.

I might be an asshole at times, but I wasn't a complete dick.

Chapter Seventeen

BOOTY CALL

Kenzie

It's Friday, and I have no plans. My life
officially sucks. Instead of going home after getting off work
early, I head to my dad's office. Too many weeks have passed
since we've properly caught up, so I'm hoping he's free for
dinner.

My mom passed away when I was twelve, and my dad
stepped up in a big way for me. He never once made me feel
like his grief was more important than me, even though I
knew just looking at me reminded him of his late wife.

The man is a saint. He even talked me through my first
period and uncomfortably taught me about safe sex and
boys before I entered high school. We'd have shopping days
and daddy-daughter dates a few times a month, which I
cherish and miss dearly with my busier adult schedule.

I park in the familiar parking garage and take the
elevator up to the nineteenth floor of the high-rise building
my dad has worked in for the last twenty years. He made

partner with his law firm after only being there a few years. I worried he would work too hard once I moved out, but he often assures me I have nothing to worry about.

When I get to his floor, I make my way to the front desk, taking note of the new abstract art on the walls and fresh flowers on the tables.

"Hi, Sherry," I say to the receptionist and offer a smile.

She looks up and tucks her brunette curls behind one ear. "Oh, McKenzie! What a lovely surprise. Does James know you're coming by?"

I shake my head. "I was hoping to catch him in a lull."

She grins and stands before smoothing her hands over her modest black dress. "Well, you're in luck. It's been a slow week with half the courthouse out sick. Follow me."

It's not necessary for her to show me to his office, but I don't tell her that. If it's been slow, then I'm sure she's just looking for something to do.

Sherry knocks on the closed door and peeks her head in.

"Hello, beautiful," I hear my dad say.

My hand covers my mouth to suppress my shock, and I don't miss the way Sherry's shoulders go rigid.

"McKenzie is here," she says quietly.

When she turns around, my hand is still on my face, but I'm grinning.

Her face is bright red, and she avoids my gaze, but I grab her hand before she can walk away. "If he's happy, then so am I."

She looks up at me with awe in her blue eyes. "Really?"

"Really."

She squeezes my hand. "Thank you."

My dad comes out of the office sheepishly, but there's a

glint in his green eyes that I don't miss. He adjusts the navy-blue tie at his neck, then runs a hand over the back of his salt-and-pepper hair. "Hey, I wasn't expecting you, but I'm glad you stopped by."

I glance between him and Sherry. "Are you sure?"

His lips flatten, and I get the "dad look" he's always been great at. "Get over here, McKenzie Jane."

Sherry walks back toward the front desk, and I head right into my dad's waiting arms. "Hi, Daddy."

"Hi, Pumpkin." His arms tighten around me before letting go and guiding me into his office. When he closes the door, he nods toward it. "The thing with Sherry. It's new or I would have told you."

I grin. "It's okay. I'm glad you're dating. It's about damn time."

He laughs and takes a seat on the couch at the back wall of his office. "Yeah, maybe."

I join him and grab his hand. "I've missed you. Sorry I've been so busy."

"It's okay. Until today, I've been pretty busy myself with a big case that just ended. The courthouse nearly being shutdown has been a blessing I didn't realize I needed," he says.

I tilt my head. "Did you win the case?"

"Of course I did. Medical malpractice where the husband died due to neglect. It was a rough one," he answers with a sigh.

My head leans against his shoulder. "I'm proud of you, Dad."

He squeezes my hand. "Just like I am of you. My

stubborn daughter who hasn't let me help her with anything besides school since she turned eighteen."

I laugh him off even though he's right. I could never take his money. Not for my apartment, or car, or anything else. The only reason he was able to call the school was because he knew all my information to call in and make the payments before me. He's always worked hard, and I've done my best to follow in his footsteps with my own career.

"This promotion has been kicking my ass," I say.

"I bet, but I know you'll do great with all these projects they have you leading. That brain of yours is probably loving all the challenges," he replies with a chuckle.

"It is most days." I look up at him. "Can you do dinner tonight? Or do you already have other plans?"

He smiles and goes to grab his briefcase from next to his desk. "I will never turn down a night with my beautiful daughter."

I glance toward the door. "If you want to invite Sherry, I'm okay with that."

"Next time. And we'll make sure not so much time has passed between dinner dates." Dad grabs my hand and leads us out the door.

We make our way to the front desk, and I wave at Sherry. She smiles and says, "Have a good evening, you two."

"Thank you, Sherry." Dad locks eyes with her, and the way he smiles makes my heart flutter with overwhelming happiness.

My dad has been alone for the most part since my mom died. I'm sure he's dated, but nothing serious, and that always made me sad for him.

"Bye, Sherry," I call out as we head to the elevators.

"I hope to see you soon, McKenzie," she replies, and I smirk. I'm sure that will happen.

I'm still grinning when the doors close. My dad is blushing. "This is a good look on you, Dad."

"Yeah. When am I going to see the same one on you?" He nudges me with his shoulder.

I laugh. "Nice deflection. Where do you want to eat?"

"Talk about deflection. Are you seeing someone?" His dark brows narrow while he attempts to give me his best lawyer stare-down.

My hesitation is answer enough, and I know I fucked up.

"Who is he? And don't tell me nobody. I know my daughter better than that," Dad says with a softening smile.

I loop my arm through his. "He's just a guy who's gotten under my skin. I'm sure it's nothing."

"Right. Well, just so you know, I was the bane of your mother's existence before she fell in love with me."

My chest tightens. I am not falling in love with Bentley Abbott. Not now and not ever.

———

THE FOLLOWING WEEK, I'M FINALLY FEELING settled in my new position and getting to know how my new team works. I've been getting home at normal hours, and there has only been one emergency after hours situation since the all-nighter I pulled the week before.

During the dinner with my dad, I'd told him about the fundraiser I'm working on, and he made a sizable donation on behalf of his law firm. I was super excited about it until I texted Bentley to tell him about it and only got a thumbs-up in reply.

Since then, I haven't reached out again, and he hadn't until today when he asked if we could do dinner.

Instead of replying to him, I text my girls.

Me: Should I accept Bentley's offer of dinner after not hearing from him for a week?

Ella: Do you want to get laid again?

Piper: Yes. Your grumpiness needs to cease.

Me: Ha! I am not grumpy. I'm all sunshine and you know it. And yes, Ella. Getting laid is never a bad thing. Duh.

Piper: Maybe, but there's an eclipse over you and for once I'm looking forward to you telling us about all the orgasms you get to have.

Ella: Maybe we need to find Piper a businessman, Kenz? So she can talk about her own orgasms...

Piper: I'm going back to my book before you two ruin my mood.

Me: Oh, Pipe. Don't get your puss all chapped. You know we love you.

Piper: GOODBYE

Ella: She's going to unfriend us. Go on the date and tell her about the orgasms later to make up for your crude comment.

I bite my lip. Maybe they're right. Or maybe I just need to stop overthinking anything to do with Bentley. His hot-and-cold personality may be driving me nuts, but if I consider him the booty call of a lifetime, things could be less complicated.

With my phone still in hand, I pull up Bentley's text and tell him yes.

Fucker: I'll pick you up at seven.

My eyes glance at the clock. I have four hours to go and spend the rest of my time at work sorting through my emails.

That's when I spot one from Bentley sent just a minute before he texted me. I quickly open it and there's nothing but business names, contact information, and dollar amounts.

Holy shit, he's raised nearly forty-thousand-dollars in the last few days for the shelter. No wonder I haven't heard from him.

Guilt trickles in along with a bit of stupidity.

Bentley isn't my boyfriend. So what if we've fucked a couple times? He's made no promises, other than not kicking me out again.

Yep. He's a booty call and nothing more. I need to keep that fact at the forefront of my thoughts when we have dinner tonight, and even more so when I let him take me home.

Chapter Eighteen

PANTIES IN A TWIST

Bentley

AFTER SEEING SELENE AT THE BAKERY AND thinking about Kenzie, I take some time to figure out what I want. Selene definitely isn't that, and while Kenzie makes my dick hard unlike anyone ever has, she's nothing like any other woman I've dated in my past.

I kept telling myself that was a bad thing, but the more I think about her, the more I realize that maybe this wild woman came into my life at just the right time.

Maybe I needed to stop being such an ass and ask her on a proper date. Something tells me this could go badly—Kenzie *is* unpredictable—but that's part of what draws me to her.

With reservations made at my favorite seafood house, I wait for Kenzie to accept my offer to dinner.

When she finally does, I let out a breath I didn't realize I was holding.

"Shit, when was the last time I was nervous over a

woman?" I mutter to myself. I don't have an answer to that question, but I am thankful that the donations and majority of the fundraiser planning are done.

This dinner isn't going to be about work. If Kenzie thinks that, I hope she realizes once she sees my email that our jobs are nearly done.

Plus, I meet with Joyce tomorrow, and I know she'll be happy to see I got my shit together. I print my email to Kenzie, and I've made sure to add the donation from her father's firm to the list with a note of credit to her.

Once I tuck that into my bag, I double-check that everything is locked up and decide to head home for the day.

"Hey, Brad," I say when I exit my office. "I'm going to be unavailable for the rest of the day. Send anything urgent to the proper department heads if something comes up."

He grins. "Sure thing, boss. Have a fun evening."

I walk away without saying anything else. He's good at his job, but a little too young for my liking. Everything is about having "fun" to him.

Though I do intend to get some tonight, that isn't something I would ever discuss in the office. Hell, not even Owen has asked me about Kenzie. At least he's a smart man, one who has been underutilized at this company for far too long.

I know the board recently promoted him, but he's already mastered the marketing department. I have plans to challenge him further, but that's a thought for another day.

Tonight is about Kenzie and hoping she doesn't laugh in my face when I tell her this is a real date and not about the fundraiser or anything else.

RIGHT AT SEVEN, I KNOCK ON KENZIE'S DOOR AND hear her laugh getting louder as she comes to the door humming a song I feel like I should know but can't place.

"Seven o'clock on the dot." She grins widely, grabs a small black purse from the hook next to the door, and locks up.

I stare at her and can't speak. She's wearing a navy-blue dress that hugs every curve and dips to her mid-back, plus black heels that can't be comfortable to walk in but are sexy as hell.

When she turns around, my eyes go to her chest, and she shimmies her shoulders. "I take your silence to mean you like?"

My head nods eagerly. "I do. You look stunning."

She gives me a slow once-over. I'm wearing gray slacks and, coincidently, my collared button-up is very close in color to her sexy dress.

Kenzie pats my cheek. "You ditched the tie and coat. I like it."

She walks toward the stairs without waiting for me, and I shake my head while a smile grows on my face.

I lengthen my stride to catch up and follow her to the passenger side of my Range Rover before opening the door for her.

Her head cocks to the side, but she doesn't comment on my actions.

I go around to the front and get in the driver's seat. The silence is already beginning to feel awkward, and I don't blame Kenzie for being confused. I was either being an asshole to her before or fucking her senseless. There wasn't much of an in between, but still, she didn't scare away easily. That's how we got to where we are now.

"Did you get my email earlier?" I ask once I pull onto the main road, then berate myself for bringing up the fundraiser when I said I wouldn't.

She nods. "I was rather impressed. You did good this week. Maybe you'll get a treat later." She winks at me, and I chuckle.

"What a lucky boy I am."

"Being in my company? Absolutely." Kenzie grins while she stares out the windshield.

I steal glances as I drive, noticing the way her fiery hair glistens under the city lights while we pass through downtown.

She catches me staring at a stop light. "Do I have something on my face?"

"Nope. Just enjoying the view."

Her cheeks blush, and when she doesn't say anything in return, I'm surprised.

We get to the restaurant, and I groan when I see how packed they are. Just because we have a reservation doesn't mean service won't still be slow thanks to the busy Thursday evening.

"I've been here once with my dad and one of his clients. Good choice," Kenzie says and gets out on her own.

I hurry around the front to meet her and do something I know she won't expect. I take her hand in mine and squeeze. "I'm glad you think so."

She gasps softly, but I don't call attention to the action.

Instead, I lead us toward the doors and stop immediately when I see camera flashes.

I haven't had to deal with the paparazzi since I cut ties with my parents. I'm not sure why they're here tonight, but it explains why the parking lot is so full.

Kenzie moves closer to me, and I let go of her hand to wrap my arm around her waist.

Keeping our heads down, we go inside, and I breathe a sigh of relief that everything is normal beyond the front doors.

"Holy shit," Kenzie mutters and I follow her gaze. A small group of A-list actors are laughing at the bar, uncaring that most of the restaurant is staring at them. At least nobody is harassing them for photos and autographs.

"Welcome, can I get your name?" the petite hostess asks.

"Bentley Abbott. I have a reservation," I say.

She browses the tablet in her hands. "Yes, Mr. Abbott. I have you right here. Follow me, please."

Thankfully, she leads us to the opposite side of the room from the celebrities. I don't want to be caught in the middle of any chaos if one of the paparazzi happens to sneak in.

I keep Kenzie at my side until we get to our table and then sit across from her. The hostess disappears and the silence returns.

"Kenzie," I say roughly.

She tilts her head. "Yes?"

"This is a date." My eyes watch her face.

She grins. "Okay. As long as it has a happy ending, then I don't mind."

My hand reaches across the table, and I settle it over hers. "I'd like to date you."

"Oh." All emotions drop from her face.

Fuck. That wasn't what I expected.

I stand my ground, though, waiting for her to process what I've said.

Finally, she blinks several times. "Why?"

I chuckle. "What do you mean 'why'?"

"We're total opposites." Her other hand gestures between the two of us. "I live in a tiny house. You have a mansion. I have a Honda. You drive a Range Rover probably worth more than my new annual salary. Different sides of the tracks, Bentley."

"So, because of all that, I'm only allowed to want to fuck you?" I raise a brow.

Her hazel eyes darken. "No, that's not what I'm saying."

"Then, what *are* you saying? Am *I* not good enough for you to date?" I challenge.

She laughs loudly, then covers her mouth to quiet the sound. "Also, wasn't what I was saying. I just mean...I thought this was only sex...and getting on each other's nerves. For however long it lasted."

I pull my hand back. "It still can be if that's what you prefer."

The disappointment I feel is hidden from my words, and I hope she can't see it on my face. I don't need a pity date.

Kenzie's fingers drum over the table. The longer she's quiet, the more I begin to appreciate that she's giving my proposal to dating some serious thought.

It reminds me of why I couldn't get her out of my head in the first place. Kenzie wouldn't be going out with me for my money or for what I can offer her. She's a stubborn, mouthy, independent woman. Everything I didn't know I wanted.

Our server comes and Kenzie is still quiet, so I order surf and turf for the both of us. When he leaves, I take a long pull of my water before breaking the silence.

"We can leave if you want."

Her eyes widen. "No. I'm sorry. I just have all these scenarios going through my head right now, and I'm not good at compartmentalizing my emotions...or with surprises."

"I see. Well, how are the scenarios working out?"

She smirks. "Most of them are coming up with never-ending orgasms."

I match her smile. "That doesn't sound terrible. For either of us."

The quietness returns, and I'm ready to ask what the other scenarios are, but before I can, she finally says, "Okay."

"Okay, what?" I want her to say the words I know she's capable of forming.

"I'll date you, but I don't need this fancy shit all the time."

I laugh darkly. "God, the things I want to do to that mouth of yours..."

She tenses from across the table, then leans back against the booth. A second later, I feel something brush against my inner thigh.

My shoulders go rigid. "Kenzie." My tone is warning, and her mood is softening by the second.

"Don't get your panties in a twist, Mr. Abbott. I wouldn't give you a foot job in public," she says not-so-quietly.

"Foot job, huh?" I question.

She wiggles her hands. "Well, these aren't reaching all the way over there."

I'm tempted to move over to her side, but that's probably a terrible idea, especially with all of the cameras outside. There's no telling what they can see from the windows.

Our food arrives, and the rest of my nerves disappear. I don't know what dating McKenzie Chase is going to be like, but I'm certain it's going to be one hell of an adventure for however long it lasts.

Chapter Nineteen

ALL THE FUCKING FUCKS

Kenzie

Well, last night didn't go at all how I expected. Except for the sex. That was hot as fuck. But Bentley asking me to basically be his girlfriend was way out of left field.

So much so that I almost told him no. I enjoy having sex with him. Before he came along, I hadn't found anyone to rock my world like he does. The thought of losing that because we put a label on things... Well, I didn't like that.

Though, as I stare at his sleeping form now, I'm thinking maybe this won't be so bad.

Bentley is my complete opposite, and I'd be lying if I said I didn't enjoy the way he challenges me. At least, most of the time.

I prop myself up on my elbow, and with the other hand, my pointer finger traces the muscles in his bicep. "Good morning, dickmatizer."

He cracks one eye open and turns a little more toward me. "What did you just call me?"

My lips quirk into a smile. "A dickmatizer."

Bentley sits up a little straighter. "Shouldn't you be the dickmatizer?"

I lean forward and capture his lips with my own. "Depends on the day. Or night."

Before he can get his incoming arm around me, I roll out of bed, and he pouts. It's an action that I find hot as fuck.

"Come back to bed," he demands, throwing back the blankets.

I give my head a shake, even though I really want to do as he says. "I need to get to work. Some of us don't run our own companies and we have to show up on time."

His legs swing off the bed, and he strides toward me, naked and proud. "Let me at least make you breakfast."

My heart warms as my head nods, even though I'm not a huge breakfast person. "What are my choices?"

He smirks and raises the back of his hand before trailing it down my side. "My recommendation is dick in bed, but we also have eggs, bagels, and cereal varieties."

This new side of Bentley, the one that's light and carefree, isn't someone I thought he was capable of being, but it's only adding to his appeal.

"As tempting as option one is, I really do need to get to work. I'll take a bagel. Toasted, please."

He grabs the back of my neck and kisses me thoroughly. "You're missing out."

Oh, don't I know it, I think as he exits the bedroom butt-ass naked.

I grab my clothes and dress quickly before grabbing a sweatshirt from Bentley's closet and his sweatpants that were neatly folded on a shelf inside the big walk-in space.

As I head downstairs, my heart is fuller than it has been in a long time. Whatever worries I had before about ruining what we had by putting a label on our relationship were hopefully nothing more than ridiculous thoughts.

———

THIRTY MINUTES LATER, BENTLEY DROPS ME OFF at home, and I hurriedly get ready for work. By the time I arrive at Global Tech, there are only a few minutes to spare. This is the latest I've shown up since I got my promotion, and though I'm not late, I feel almost guilty.

Waiting at my desk is Glen. I haven't really talked to him since the day my promotion was announced.

"Good morning, Glen," I say and sidestep him to get in my door. "Can I help you?"

He adjusts his clip-on tie, but it's still crooked. "You're late with the write-up for the Parson project."

Oh, this dude. He is way out of his depth right now, and I'm about to show him that.

I smile sweetly. "Actually, thanks to a misstep from your department—that I didn't bring major notice to—Joslin extended that deadline to next week and Parsons already approved. You must have missed that email, just like you forgot to include the data breach protection to the file you sent through the test run."

His mouth opens and closes like a fish, and I shoo him

away with my hand. "Now, if you'll excuse me, I have work to do."

He mutters something unintelligible on his way out, and I log into my computer.

Serves that fucker right for coming in here and trying to catch me slipping up. I'd never rub someone else's shortcomings in their face normally, but he asked for it when he tried to do the same to me.

Speaking of fucker... I still had plenty of thoughts about *my* fucker and our shared dinner. Just yesterday, I was content to have him as my booty call, and now we are officially dating? I don't understand how that happened so quickly.

Me: Bentley asked me to be his girlfriend last night.

I send the text to Ella and Piper, hoping they'll have some insight.

Ella: Congrats! I told you he seemed like a nice guy.

Piper: Did you tell him yes?

I laugh at Piper's response. She knows me so well.

Me: I did.

Piper: And how do you feel about that?

And there's the golden question.

Me: I don't know. I thought one thing and then he completely threw a curve ball at me.

Ella: Take a lesson from my book. There's nothing wrong with just seeing how things work out. Don't overthink whatever happened last night. If you were intending to keep fucking him anyway, what's the difference?

My knee bounces rapidly as I try to find an answer. If I thought I could have kept screwing Bentley and not have grown more feelings for him, I was out of my mind. Ella is right. There's not much different, except now things are just a bit more official.

Piper: Holy shit. Google Bentley Abbott. Right. Now.

A video call starts in group chat, and I ignore it until I do as Piper asked. Well, demanded.

Fucking fuck.

My face is on Google. With Bentley. At that restaurant last night.

How? Why? When?

I'm sitting there, smiling at Bentley, and the way he's gazing at me hits me right in the chest. How did I miss that intensity during dinner?

I finally answer the video call, but I'm speechless.

"Did you know someone was taking pictures of you?" Ella asks as soon as my face appears on the screen.

I shake my head. "There were celebrities there. We thought the paparazzi was just paying attention to them."

Piper whistles. "I knew Bentley was rich from what you'd told me, but damn, Kenz. His family is huge in the business world in New York. No wonder they took interest. These pictures were posted in a magazine up there."

Shit. I wonder if Bentley knew. And if he did, did he care? Would this upset him? Maybe I shouldn't say anything. He's always been private, and honestly, there's nothing wrong with the picture. We're just having dinner.

Ella bites her lip. "Check out the article."

A couple clicks later, some cheeseball slander site pops

up. It takes closing out of three ads before I can see what they wrote.

Lost Prodigal Son Resurfaces in North Carolina

Bentley Abbott left New York six years ago and, from what we know, he's never been back. Is there a story there we've been missing all along? Quite possibly given that finance mogul Morgan Abbott never speaks of his first heir. Yet, their daughter Celia still visits and proudly appears at her parents' side when called upon.
The world might have forgotten about Abbott's first child, but as we can all see, he's alive and well. Maybe this spotting means it's time to dust off the detective hat and see what, or better yet, who, chased Bentley away all those years ago.
For now, we can all ponder who the lucky lady is that's captured this billionaire's heart. Will she last, or is this just a fling we shouldn't concern ourselves with?
To be continued...

All the fucking fucks.

Bentley is going to lose his shit. I might not know him well, but I know enough to understand he's going to want to murder someone.

"Are you okay, Kenz?" Piper asks softly.

I stare at my phone, taking in both of my friends' concerned faces. "Yeah, I should probably call Bentley, though."

Ella frowns. "This might be better news delivered in person. Can you leave work?"

I can if I work late tonight...

Absolutely worth it, even if it's Friday.

I nod. "I'll catch up with you ladies later today."

"Good luck," Piper calls out just as I end the chat.

Quickly, I scan my emails and the files on my desk. There's nothing urgent, so I head down to Joslin's office. Clara is there and she smiles up at me. "How can I help you, McKenzie?"

"I was hoping to speak with Joslin for a minute," I say, crossing my fingers behind my back that she's in a good mood this morning.

Clara frowns. "She's not in this morning. She won't be back until this afternoon."

Oh. Well, I could leave and she'd never know. No, I can't do that.

"That's okay. I'll just send her an email." At least I can't get in trouble for not telling her I took off.

I pull my phone out of my purse and type out an email to Joslin, promising to work late in order to make up for the missed time. Hopefully, I'm back before she returns at least.

I hurry downstairs and to the parking lot. Within minutes, I'm in my car and heading toward West-to-East, Inc. The last time I showed up there, I was trying to piss off Bentley. Now, I'm hoping like hell he won't care what those stupid magazines have to say and that my first thought about him being pissed would be wrong.

I know nothing about his family history. Maybe this won't be a big deal. Yeah, I need to think positive.

Or I could be realistic and understand that this could change everything. God, I hope not.

Too many minutes later, I've begun to spiral with all of

the "what ifs" on why Bentley would have left New York. My stomach is churning.

Have I been fucking a psycho? Honestly, I wouldn't be surprised. Not because of Bentley, either. That's just my luck some days.

I make my way to Bentley's office. None of the employees seem overly nervous, so that must mean their CEO hasn't gone on a rampage. That should make me feel better, but it doesn't.

Brad, Bentley's assistant, waves at me when he spots me coming down the hallway. "Hey, Kenzie."

I smile. "Is Bentley busy?"

As I ask the question, Owen comes out of his office, leaving the door cracked. He doesn't smile, and I take that to mean he's still pissed about the dinner I interrupted.

"You didn't like my peace offering?" I ask him with a waggle of my brows.

"I'd have rather you not barged into my house," he replies, folding his arms over his chest.

I walk up to him and pat his shoulder. "You asked for this when you asked my best friend to marry you. We're a package deal, O. If you didn't understand that before, I don't know what to tell you."

He shakes his head. "What are you doing here?"

"I need to talk to Bentley." I drop my arm and try to peek inside the office, but I can't see the man in question.

Owen raises a brow. "About?"

"Things. If he didn't tell you, then I'm not going to, either," I say quietly, even though I know he'll know everything with one call to Ella.

Owen had to accept Piper and me as a package deal

with Ella, and we had to accept that our best friend's soon-to-be husband would know our secrets as well. At least the ones he might outright ask about.

Bentley appears in the doorway, and his lips twitch but don't quite raise. His ability to always appear like an asshole is almost endearing now that I know him better.

"Kenzie," he says evenly.

I give him my full attention as my stomach churns again. "Do you have a few minutes?"

He looks at Owen. "You have everything you need, right?"

Owen nods. "I'll take care of it."

Bentley shakes his hand. "Thank you." Then, he gestures for me to enter.

I wave at Brad, who has quietly witnessed all of our conversations without saying much. I then wonder how much all the assistants around the office hear and what they do with said information. I picture them like maids, meeting in the breakroom and swapping gossip.

The thought makes me snort, and that earns me a glower from Bentley. "Something funny?"

I frown as he shuts the door behind him. "Actually, no. I'm not sure how you're going to feel about this, so I'll just show it to you."

Bentley's chest expands, and his shoulders go rigid while I pull up the article on my phone. When I hand it to him, he lets out a sigh of relief.

"Jesus, I thought you were going to show me a pregnancy test." His hand squeezes the back of his neck.

I laugh. "No, but good to know you'd panic about that."

I'm not even sure he hears what I've said, because his grip tightens around my phone while he reads the article on the screen.

"How did you find this?" he asks through gritted teeth.

I take a step closer. "I was on the phone with my friends. Piper found it. Not sure what she was looking for in the first place, but..."

He takes a shuddering breath, and I reach for his arm. "Is this going to cause problems for you?"

Bentley looks down at me. His jaw is still tense, but his eyes are softening. "Not directly. I have nothing to hide, but my parents might have issue. That's not of my concern, though. Not anymore."

He hands me the phone back and storms back to his desk.

I follow and take a seat in the chair across from him, giving him some space. "Want to talk about it?"

His icy eyes land on me. "There's nothing to talk about."

I chuckle. "You're such a man. An online magazine, no matter how sleezy or irreputable, is talking about digging into your family, and I can see the murder on your face. There is absolutely something to talk about."

He leans his head back against the chair and stares at the ceiling. "Is this what I signed up for, asking to date you? Inquisitiveness and caring?"

Bentley might not be smiling, but his tone is softer, and I don't take offense to his questions.

Instead, I get up and walk around his desk, then move his arms out of my way and sit on his lap. "Yep. Do you have a problem with that?"

He looks at me and finally grins. "Surprisingly, no."

"Good. Now, tell me about your family in case I get cornered in the street somewhere by crazy reporters."

His glower returns, and I make a mental note to keep my sarcasm to a minimum for this particular topic.

Chapter Twenty

RUIN ME

Bentley

HAVING THIS CONVERSATION WITH KENZIE SO soon wasn't in the plans, but since the bottom-feeders from last night realized who I was, I can't leave her in the dark.

"Our family isn't famous or anything, but my father has made a name for himself in the financial district. When there's nothing exciting to lie about with the celebrities, the leeches head down to Wall Street. Thanks to a couple of nights out with my friends when I was too young to know better, I caught their attention a time or two. Not that I was doing anything wrong, but that's part of the reason why I don't speak to my parents anymore."

Kenzie watches me with trepidation. "What happened between you guys?"

My palm rubs over her thigh. "My mother is a socialite. The things you see on reality TV and in the movies about rich women? They have nothing on what goes on in real life. It's cutthroat and dirty and asinine most of the time.

My mother threatened to sue me if I ended up in the papers again."

Her jaw drops. "Sue you for what?"

"Defamation of the family name." I laugh, because there's nothing more I can do at this point. "I confirmed then what I already knew to be true in my heart. My parents cared more about their image and the size of their bank account than they did their children who were raised more by rotating nannies than anyone else."

Kenzie leans against my shoulder. "I'm sorry that happened to you, but it seems like you've done well on your own."

I nod. "My grandmother on my dad's side was nothing like my mother. In fact, she hated my mom. Unfortunately, since my grandmother didn't hide her disdain, I didn't get to see her much. When she died and left me her house here, I knew I had the out I needed. I packed up my shit and left. My sister followed me when she was done with school. Though I never asked her to do that, I'm glad she did in her own way that allowed her to stay in our parents' good graces."

Kenzie cringes. "Now I feel bad for mocking your huge house. I told myself you were compensating."

My fingers brush her hair back. "I didn't think I had a reason to do that."

She shrugs. "You don't, but after you'd kicked me out, I made myself believe that you did."

I wish our conversation could end there, on a good note, but I'm not done.

"My mother leaked to the press that I'd left New York to spend time at a treatment center. Thankfully, when they couldn't find me or proof of where I was, not even the gossip sites picked up the leak. I've been living my own life, away from the deep-pocket circles ever since. But if one of those bottom-feeders does corner you, know that they'll likely ask questions about things that aren't true in an attempt to trip you up or turn you against me."

Her hand settles over my heart, warming my chest. "I'm not one to believe what I see or read online, and I'm sure the hell not going to trust anything a complete stranger says just so they can get a reaction out of me."

"Thank you." I tighten an arm around her. "My life normally doesn't have any drama in it. In fact, I ended things with my last ex to avoid falling back into that lifestyle. She began to remind me too much of my mother."

I shudder, and Kenzie laughs. "Well, I never took my father's money, and I don't intend to find an interest in yours, so you don't have to worry about that with me."

My hand cups her cheek. "If I thought that, I wouldn't have shared any of this with you."

Her eyes heat, and the distance between us is quickly closed when she presses her lips against mine, then murmurs, "Should we christen your office?"

I dig my fingers into her hips and turn her until she's straddling me. "I wish, but I have meetings I can't avoid, and you're probably supposed to be at work yourself, given how much of a hurry you were in this morning."

Her lower lip juts out. "I don't like it when you're right."

"I'll be all kinds of wrong for you tonight to make up for it." I kiss her again, letting our tongues greet each other. She moans into my mouth and presses down on my lap.

Fuck, I want to take her right here on my desk, but even if I chose to blow off the meeting, I don't have a condom. That's something I intend to rectify for the future.

Regrettably, I push Kenzie back. "No protection, and we both need to work."

"You ruin all the fun." She leans against my desk and pushes out her chest.

I lift her up, thankful she's wearing a dress today. Her ass thuds on the desk's sleek surface and I spread her legs apart. Before she realizes what I'm doing, I have two fingers buried inside her.

"How's this for fun?" I whisper in her ear.

Her back curves, and she inches closer to me. "Terrible."

"Lies." I nip at her neck, and she moans. My other hand covers her mouth while my fingers curl inside her.

I move in and out of her wet pussy, and she groans louder, then bites down on my hand when her body shudders.

"Shhh," I growl in her ear, but I don't relent. I work my hand harder, enjoying how drips of her pleasure trail down my fingers. "Come for me, Kenzie. Right here, right now."

Her head nods within my hold, and her eyes squeeze closed.

My thumb presses against her clit and she bucks against me. Something unintelligible leaves her mouth, and I replace my hand with my lips, kissing her mouth as she comes all over my other hand and the top of my desk.

"Motherfucking hell, Bentley. Give a girl a warning next time," she heaves, trying to catch her breath and resting her head against my shoulder.

I grin against her cheek. "What fun would that be?"

I slowly pull my fingers out of her pussy, and she shudders again. I bring my hand up and lick my pointer finger. "That will have to hold me over until tonight."

Kenzie sucks in a breath. "You're going to ruin me."

"Good." My hand grabs the back of her neck, and I claim her mouth again, inhaling her sweet scent.

I didn't want to care about this woman, but she wormed her way in the moment she spilled her drink on me, along with every word spoken and action taken since then.

If I ruin her for every other man in this world, then I'll consider that a conquest worth celebrating.

THE NEXT COUPLE WEEKS GO BY WITHOUT incident. There are no other articles to worry about, and I haven't seen a camera pointed in my direction once. Kenzie and I have settled into taking turns staying at each other's house, and the sex... Somehow, it's only gotten more addictive.

Tonight, though, she's meeting my sister, and I'm actually nervous.

Celia has been bugging me about dinner since I warned her about the paparazzi, and I didn't cave until this week. To make things less awkward, Kenzie suggested that we invite her friends and Owen over, too.

I wasn't sure about that, but now that the night is upon us, I'm thankful it won't just be my sister grilling my girlfriend.

The doorbell rings, and Kenzie is already downstairs. "I got it."

The next sound I hear is a couple of squeals, and I'm glad I stayed in the bedroom for an extra moment. By the time I make it down, Kenzie has her arm looped through the one of a dark brunette with glasses. I assume she's Piper since I've met Ella a couple times now.

I clear my throat, and they both turn around. Piper's light-green eyes appraise me, and they widen just slightly. She's dressed up more than I expected in a dark-brown dress, boots with several-inch-tall heels, and a cream scarf around her neck.

She smiles and waves. "I'm Piper."

I offer a slight bow of my head. "Nice to officially meet you finally, Piper. I'm Bentley."

There's another knock at the door, and this time I answer it. Owen and Ella are on the other side, and my shoulders sag a little in relief, knowing I won't be the only man present for this little dinner.

I shake Owen's hand. "Glad you could make it."

"I wouldn't leave you alone with these three. I've been subject to that for months now." He feigns a shudder, and Ella backhands him in the stomach.

"You love every minute of it." Ella hugs me. "Thanks for having us. At least this time we won't be interrupted by conversations about your...body parts."

"Ella," Owen practically growls.

She shrugs. "What? He's dating Kenzie. There's no way he's *that* sensitive, and we're not at your work. Here, we're friends. Right, Bentley?"

I offer Owen a sympathetic smile before answering. "Of course."

As they step inside, I spot my sister's car pulling up. Seems everyone is going to be right on time tonight. Which is good, because neither Kenzie or I are fans of cooking and we had Chinese food brought in. This way, it won't have a chance to get cold.

Ella and Owen join the others while I wait for my sister. She half jogs up to the door and throws her arms around me with a massive smile on her face.

"What has you so happy?" I ask.

She glances behind me and whispers, "Um, hello! I'm meeting your girlfriend. I've never done that before, besides Selene. But she doesn't count, because I knew her first. This is a day to be celebrated. I even brought wine."

My sister swivels her massive purse around, and I see three corks peeking out. "Take it easy and don't embarrass me, Celia."

She pats my chest. "Of course not. I'm sure you do enough of that on your own. Now where is she?"

Celia pushes past me and locks eyes on Kenzie. Slow smiles build on both of their faces, and I know I'm in trouble. Kenzie steps away from her friends and heads to meet Celia whose arms are open.

They embrace tightly and sway back and forth. "I'm so glad to finally meet you," Celia says excitedly.

"Same. Now that we've made it happen, we'll have to make it a regular occurrence," Kenzie offers, and I barely manage to stifle my groan.

I look at Owen, and he shrugs as if to say, *You're fucked, dude. Just accept it.*

Though, deep down, I'm not fucked at all. I know that even if these women end up driving me crazy by getting together however often they want, I'll love every moment of it.

This is what I didn't have growing up: friends and family that actually gave a shit about each other and not just what they could gain from socializing together.

Kenzie lets go of my sister and steps to my side. "Do you guys mind if we do dinner first? Then, if anyone wants to snoop around the big mansion, I can take them on a tour." She winks at me. "I've done it enough to feel like an expert."

I wrap an arm around her. "Of course, you have."

Celia claps her hands, then gasps. "Oh, and I brought dessert. I hope that was okay."

Kenzie leans closer to her, face dead serious. "Please tell me you brought the dick cookies I've been hearing about."

"There's no better after-dinner treat." Celia grins widely.

"I knew I was going to love your sister." Kenzie gives me a quick kiss, then goes back to Celia. "Come meet my friends."

Owen circles wide around them and joins me. "I'm just glad I'm not on my own in this anymore."

"You could have warned me," I say jokingly.

He holds his hands up innocently. "You got yourself into this all on your own. I made a vow not to let any of Ella's friends date my co-workers, but maybe this won't be so bad."

I nod. "Yeah, maybe not."

Chapter Twenty-One

ROPES AND WHIPS AND HANDCUFFS

Kenzie

It's quite possible that I'm going to fall in love with two Abbotts. Celia is a doll, and I've already inducted her into our circle with promises for lunch soon. Even Ella and Piper seemed to like her, and it's not often we meet someone all three of us approve of.

After sharing a few drinks and laughing over shared stories, Bentley and I finally say goodbye to our guests. It's getting late, but I'm not at all tired when he locks the door after seeing Celia out.

When he turns around, I'm leaning against the banister. He prowls toward me, his hands reaching for me before he's even close.

My pussy immediately perks up, but instead of whisking me into his arms and taking me to the bedroom, Bentley bends down and whispers in my ear. "In all your sleuthing, did you find the roof patio?"

I pull back with wide eyes. "Excuse me? Where is this glorious-sounding place?"

He takes my hand and guides me toward the opposite side of the house. I know there are a few bedrooms, a secondary staircase, and an unused office, or possibly an old library, but I've never seen a door to the outside.

We go into the office, and he grins back at me. "Ready for this?"

I give him an "are you kidding me?" look, and he laughs.

"Follow me." Bentley pushes against one of the shelves, and the wood makes a clicking noise before popping open.

He slides the shelf out of the way and reveals a small room that's nearly empty. Only one bookcase remains with a couple of small boxes on it.

"Um, why aren't you using this space? You could knock out another wall and make it a secret sex room. Oh, my God. We have to do that. I know you're a kinky fucker. Don't tell me the idea doesn't intrigue you," I say, already picturing all of the toys this man could destroy me with.

His head shakes, but there's an interest in his lightening eyes. "We already have a sex room. It's called the bedroom."

"But it doesn't have ropes and whips and handcuffs and..."

Bentley's mouth covers mine and shuts me right up. "Do you want to see the patio or not?"

I nod, my nose brushing against his since he hasn't backed away.

"Good choice."

When Bentley takes a step forward, I finally see a steel

rung ladder secured to the wall, and my eyes follow it up to find a trap door that's already open.

I eye him suspiciously while fighting a huge grin. "What are you up to, Mr. Abbott?"

He smacks my ass. "Go on up and find out."

Not needing to be told twice, I file away my plans for a sex room and grab on to the ladder. Bentley's right behind me, and I pause before I get to the top. His head bumps into my ass and he bites down. Hard.

I look back and wink. "Like I said, kinky fucker."

I swear he mutters something that sounds a lot like "I'll show you kinky fucker," but instead of focusing on him any longer, I pay attention to making sure I don't fall back down the ladder as I climb out the top.

When I stand up and have my feet firmly planted on concrete, I look around and cover my mouth in a gasp. There are tiny lights strung around the square space, an oversized lounge couch, and a small propane firepit.

On my second sweep, I see a circular table next to the sofa, and there's a tray of strawberries and chocolate sitting there.

Bentley's arms wrap around my waist. "What do you think?"

"I think I'm in shock. Did you do all this?" I ask, still soaking in the little slice of heaven he's been hiding from me.

"I did the little stuff, but I paid the delivery company to get the couch up here while we were at work. I thought it would be a good place to come and unwind."

I laugh. "You have a ten-thousand-square-foot house. We could have relaxed anywhere inside."

He leans closer, resting his chin on my shoulder. "But I wanted something special. For you."

My heart constricts. This is a side of Bentley I normally only see the tiniest glimpses of and for brief moments. I think I could get used to the romantic buried deep beneath the grumpy, handsome man that most people see.

I wrap my arms around his neck and push up on my toes. "Am I softening the hard shell around your heart, Mr. Abbott?"

His forehead presses against mine. "I believe you are, Ms. Chase."

Bentley gets out his phone, taps on the screen a few times, then sets it on a small table. A slow song comes on with a sweet melody that instantly makes my hip sway.

His hands grip my sides, and he pulls me closer. "Thank you for tonight and for not telling me to fuck off when I was being a dick before."

I chuckle. "I wouldn't thank me for that. I thought about it plenty of times, but fortunately for me, you're really good in bed. I couldn't resist coming back when your dick asked so nicely."

He smiles down at me, and the action steals all the air around me while he twirls me around on the rooftop. I squeal and smile and feel my heart swelling.

The action is foreign for me. No man has ever taken my breath away or captured my attention like Bentley does. Even when he was infuriating me, I wanted him more than I believed I should.

One of his hands slides to my lower back, and the other takes one of mine into its grasp before resting against his chest. We stay silent, enjoying the soft hum of music, the stars above, and more importantly, each other.

I lean my head against his chest, and he presses me closer. My breathing evens, and I know right then that I could spend the rest of my days in this man's strong arms. It's a thought that terrifies me and excites me all at the same time.

When the song ends, he guides me to a lounge chair and lays down first before settling me in next to him. His arm holds me tightly to his side and I look up at his handsome face.

"Tell me something about you," I say.

His brow furrows. "Like what?"

"What's your favorite thing to do when you're not working?"

Bentley stares up at the sky before answering. "Fishing... I think."

"You think? How do you not know?" I laugh softly.

He shrugs. "I don't do much of anything besides work or volunteer, but I didn't think you'd accept that as an answer. The last time I purposely went and did something that wasn't either of those things was fishing."

I tilt my head. "Why did you choose fishing when you could have done anything else?"

He frowns. "I'd never done it before. I used to ask my dad to take me when my other friends talked about going with theirs, but he always told me that smart men didn't get their hands dirty like that."

My blood boils on Bentley's behalf. "Your dad is a fuckwad, and I'm glad you finally cut ties with them and went on to live your own life. My mom and I used to join my dad during the summers for fishing, but he stopped going after she died."

His fingers squeeze tighter around me. "How did she die?"

I take a deep breath and stare up at the night sky. "When I was eleven, she got diagnosed with cancer. Stage four in both lungs. Caught us all off guard. We at least had time to say goodbye over the following couple months. I'm not sure it helped, but I like to think so. Maybe not for my dad. He struggled a lot the last several weeks, but once she was gone, he found his way back to me and kicked ass at being both Dad and Mom for the next seven years before I headed off to college."

I'm smiling even though tears fill my eyes. I haven't spoken of my mother's death in a long time. At least, not out loud. Death isn't something most people are comfortable talking about, but once you've experienced it, there's no forgetting the helplessness you feel when it strikes.

Bentley wipes the stray tears from my cheek. "You're one hell of a woman, you know that, McKenzie Chase?"

I smirk. "I have to be to put up with you."

He shakes his head. "Insufferable as well."

I poke his ribs. "You wouldn't have me any other way. Don't try to pretend otherwise."

He surprises me when he lifts me up and over his lap. I straddle his hips, and he smiles up at me. "Tell me something else about you."

I raise my hand and tap my chin as I think. "I wanted to be a fashion designer when I went to college, but after the first semester, I changed my degree to Computer Science after only signing up for a coding class because someone told me it was easy and would satisfy some of the credits I needed."

His head cocks to the side, then he nods. "I can see that. What else?"

"My favorite color is orange, because it reminds me of the sun rising and setting every day. My favorite food is pizza. I don't like the rain, but I can tolerate the snow. Reality TV is the dumbest thing man ever thought of."

He chuckles. "I agree with that last part, but then again, I'm not a fan of any TV. I can do movies on occasion, but that's about all the screen time I can take. Green used to be my favorite color, but—" his fingers tug lightly at my hair, "—auburn is beginning to take its place. Seafood is my favorite food. Any kind. And I love the rain. At least the way the air smells after a storm. There's something calming about the silence it brings, too."

I grin widely. Our night has taken a turn I didn't expect. This side of Bentley is dangerous, and I'm glad he's kept it hidden from me for all these weeks. Though, I won't soon forget our time up here and no time will be soon enough for us to come back.

"What?" he asks with a pinched expression.

I smooth the lines between his eyes with my thumb. "I'm glad I'm here with you. That's all."

He grips my hips, eyes smoldering. "Me too."

I lean closer and press my lips to his, then whisper, "Thank you for sharing those things with me."

He holds me tighter. "Of course."

I move back to his side and rest my head on his chest,

listening to the sound of Bentley's heartbeat while staring up at the stars.

Big feelings are growing inside me and, for once, I don't want to distract them with sarcasm or sex. Instead, I immerse myself in the moment. Being here with Bentley, seeing what he's created just for us, hearing more about who he is behind the suit, satisfies me just as much as when he's screwing me senseless.

Chapter Twenty-Two

ASS. HOLE.

Bentley

AFTER SPENDING THE LAST SEVERAL WEEKS WITH Kenzie, I keep waiting for the time to come when I grow tired of her constant company, but it's the nights when she's not with me that I find myself restless.

Kenzie is the bright light in my life that I wasn't looking for. She makes fun of me when I'm grumpy instead of being offended by my sour mood. She pushes me to do things I wouldn't normally, like skinny dipping in my own heated pool and fucking her on the steps until she screamed my name. Twice.

Even my sister has grown fond of Kenzie. Since our shared dinner, I've seen them texting in the evenings and as much as I've gotten annoyed with the distractions, I'm also grateful. Celia is my only family now, and I don't know how I'd handle things if they didn't get along.

Owen walks into my office holding the new marketing

presentation samples for one of our subsidiaries. "Ready for our meeting?"

I wave him in. "Of course. Have a seat."

One thing I admire about Owen most is that he almost never brings up personal things when we're at work. I worried for a moment that Kenzie being best friends with his fiancée would become a complication, but if anything, things have only gotten better at work, as well as outside of West-to-East, Inc.

Owen takes a seat and starts spreading the drawings out. I see three different versions of branding: classic styling with standard coloring and smooth strokes, black and gray with small pops of color to draw the eyes, and then there's one I didn't expect—pop art.

I snag the last one and hold it closer. The drawing is bold and almost obnoxious, but I don't hate it.

"Why this one?" I hand the piece back to Owen.

"Sampson's is more than a grocer. They have history in neighborhoods with a variety of people. I felt this gave a classic-yet-modern style to their branding that showcases who they are." He points to the first drawing. "This one also fits well if the latter is too bold."

I shake my head. "No, I think you're onto something. Keep going with the pop art, and don't worry about checking in with me on any of these projects. You know what you're doing, but at the same time, you should also look for someone to replace you."

Owen freezes while gathering the papers. "Excuse me? I don't understand."

I smile and lean back in my chair. "This company has

never had a proper vice president. I assume that's thanks to the prior CEO, but I'd like to change that. I already talked to the board, and they all agreed that you'd make an excellent candidate. Obviously, it's not set in stone, but if you're interested, I'd like to officially present the position to them. I need more help directing the department heads. I don't want to live to work, and I wouldn't expect you to, either. If we split the workload, we should have more time to do as we please."

A heavy breath escapes him. "I didn't see that coming."

I laugh. "You weren't supposed to. Consider it, and let me know what you think next week. Everything is running fine now, but I'm always looking for ways to make things better for everyone."

"And that's why I'm glad you're in that chair instead of anyone else," Owen says with a smile, then begins gathering the papers again.

I stand and walk him to the door. "We'll talk soon."

He nods and waves before heading back to his office.

When I turn around, Brad is sitting there, staring hesitantly at me. "Kenzie called. She said she's running behind and will have to meet you at Resolutions for the meeting instead of beforehand for lunch."

"Cancel the reservation then, and please order me something from Mario's," I say, then head back into my office. No sense in leaving for food if I won't be joined by Kenzie.

Today is an important meeting for the fundraiser, though. Hopefully, she can get whatever is today's dumpster fire put out before it's time to leave.

Joyce has been emailing everyone daily providing progress reports and asking for updates. Thankfully, nothing has gone wrong, and we have more donations and ticket sales than I've ever seen. Splitting the carnival into two parts was a great idea that seems to be paying off.

Hell, one of the other board members even got a band to come play, and I was able to get the radio stations and newspapers to run a few ads and articles about the event for free.

The only unfortunate part about it all was that my name ended up on that damn online gossip website again. I haven't seen any new pictures surfacing, but that doesn't mean whoever has been writing about me isn't still keeping closer tabs than I like.

Glancing at the clock, I still have two hours before I need to leave for the shelter and a pile of paperwork that requires more of my attention than bottom-feeder, wannabe reporters.

I grab the first file and get to work, making the best use of my time.

———

I WAIT OUTSIDE THE SHELTER FOR KENZIE, BUT she hasn't answered any of my texts or calls. I'm tempted to call her work until Joyce finally comes out, tugging on my arm.

"I called my daughter. Kenzie is on her way, but she left her phone on her desk. Come on in and we'll get started."

I glance down at her with an inquisitive look. "How'd you know I was waiting for her?"

She laughs. "I'm not senile. Why do you think I paired the two of you up? You did exactly what I hoped for. It's been far too long since you've had a proper reason to smile, my boy."

The way "my boy" falls so naturally from her lips fills an empty space in my chest. I reach for her without thinking and hug her tightly. "Thank you, Joyce."

I'm thanking her for so much more than sticking her nose into my business, and I hope she knows it.

She pats my back softly. "You're welcome. Now come on. We've got a lot to do this afternoon."

Joyce teeters a little when she turns to walk back inside, so I grab her elbow. "Easy there. Are you okay?

She waves me off and steadies herself. "Nothing more than old lady syndrome. You'll be here one day. Enjoy your youth while you still can."

Her following laughter alleviates some of my unease. I don't like the thought of Joyce getting old, but her words are also a reminder that life goes by too quickly and I'm thankful for the recent changes in mine.

Thinking about Kenzie again, I give one last glance to the road before following Joyce inside. At least I know she's on her way now.

The dogs and cats are noisier than usual today, but I ignore them and head to the meeting room. Joyce is already sitting at the head of the table, and I take my normal seat next to her.

She taps her pen on the plastic tabletop. "We're less than two weeks away from the carnival. I know you all have been working hard in your spare time and it shows. We're ahead of schedule on everything, but this meeting is to make sure all of our puppies are where they should be. Sandy, how about you start?"

Sandy adjusts her glasses and reads from her notepad, going on about the list of games and events that will be happening the day of.

Next up is Dakota with pricing and ticket sales, followed by Mary going over scheduling for the bigger items like the music and pony rides.

Joyce turns to me. "Can you cover all of the items you and Kenzie worked on together?"

I nod. "Of course. We will have two food trucks and a beverage truck that will serve smoothies and sodas during the day before adding beer to the evening menu. The food trucks promised to be there all day, which helps to assure that people aren't drinking on empty stomachs if we can help it. Kenzie confirmed schedules with all three vendors just yesterday via email that I was copied on."

"And donations?" Joyce asks next.

"All promised monies have been received and deposited into the fundraiser account as of yesterday. We exceeded our pre-carnival goal by thirty thousand." I watch Joyce's face, because this is something I hadn't shared with her yet.

Tears well up and quickly fall down her cheeks. She reaches for my hand and squeezes hard. "I knew you'd do great being more hands-on with this. Thank you, Bentley."

My chest constricts. "You don't have to thank me. I'm glad I could help."

Kenzie rushes into the room, and all eyes fall on her. "I'm so sorry."

She looks frazzled and crazed. Our eyes lock and she

gives me a slight head shake, telling me that something happened, but we're not going to talk about it *yet*.

Joyce gives Kenzie a wide smile with her eyes still glistening. "It's okay, dear. I talked to Joslin." Joyce grabs another sheet of paper. "Now, we need to finalize what volunteers are working what stations. I know we have some requests, so let's see if we can make those work."

She goes on and on about how many people we need for each task, but I'm having a hard time listening. Kenzie's chest is still heaving, and she won't look at me.

I've never seen her this shaken, and I'm not okay with it. Not in the slightest. My hands tighten into fists under the table and thoughts of pummeling whoever—or whatever—upset her into nothingness fills my mind.

Kenzie gives her opinions on the volunteers, especially the ones she's recruited herself, like Ella and Piper and some co-workers.

I try to listen and be helpful, but nothing I try gets Kenzie's scared eyes out of my mind.

The meeting finally ends, and Joyce is smiling. "Thank you all so much for your efforts this year. This is already our best event yet and it hasn't even officially begun. Now, let's hope we find perfect homes for all of our deserving animals out there, so we can make room for more furry friends who need our help."

Kenzie is smiling again, but I'm not. I get up once we're dismissed and grab her hand, leading her out the door.

"I wanted to talk with Joyce and make sure she knows I didn't mean to be so late," Kenzie says, trying to slow me down, but I won't be stopped.

"She knows." My voice is deep and rumbly, something

it hasn't been since I stopped fighting my feelings for this woman.

Her other hand grabs my bicep. "Bentley."

I turn back to her and see her frown, but I don't want to stop yet. I need her alone, so I can properly wrap her up in my arms and make sure she's okay.

My feet continue to guide us outside, and I take her to the driver's side of my Range Rover since that's furthest away from the entrance to the shelter.

I grip her face and press my lips to hers, just needing to feel her. The chaste contact only eases some of my worries.

She kisses me back and wraps her arms around my waist. "Are you okay?"

I chuckle darkly. "I should be asking you that. What happened before you got here?"

Her head leans against my chest, and I see her eyes flutter close. "It's just been a shit day. I was so frustrated with one of the teams I'm working with. They messed up one of the programs to the point I almost had to start all the way over to undo the chaos. Then, I realized what time it was and grabbed my purse without realizing my phone wasn't in it."

That doesn't seem bad enough to cause the look I'd seen on her face earlier.

"What else happened?" I press.

She sighs and shudders. "While I was driving here, I already knew I was going to be late, and I might have honked at someone who was paying more attention to their phone than the traffic lights. Well, he didn't like that and followed me while honking his own horn for longer than I was comfortable with. I thought about calling the cops, but that was when I realized I'd forgotten my phone. It's fine now. I swear."

Fuck, no wonder she looked terrified when she walked in. Road-rage drivers could be unpredictable, and there is no way to be sure that maniac isn't still out there waiting for Kenzie to get back on the road. I need to be absolutely sure that isn't the case.

I hug her again, needing to feel her close to me. "I'm so sorry, Kenzie. I'll follow you back to work just to make sure nothing else happens."

She bites her lip and looks back up at me. "Do you really think it's something to worry about?"

Shit. I've only freaked her out more, which wasn't at all my intention.

My hand soothes her back. "Nothing for you to worry about any longer. I'm sure it was just some asshole having a bad day."

She laughs and pulls away enough to look up at me. "You would know, wouldn't you?"

I squeeze my arms tighter around her waist. "Watch that mouth of yours before I fill it."

Her eyes glaze over, and she licks her lips. "Ass. Hole."

A rumble builds in my chest. "You better get in your car before I put you in the back of mine."

She glances around. "If we weren't at the shelter, I'd absolutely take you up on that."

I know she would, too. That's part of the reason I'm so fucking attracted to her. She reminds me to live again.

Kenzie grabs my suit coat and raises up onto her tiptoes. "See you soon."

Her lips meet mine, and I grab her ass, holding her close for just a second longer.

"See you really soon," she amends before sashaying back to her car.

I quickly get in mine and wait for her to back up before I follow.

At least for tonight, I'm not letting her out of my sight for longer than I can help it.

Chapter Twenty-Three

A LITTLE DILDO NEVER HURT ANYONE

Kenzie

Sure enough, Bentley followed me to my work, and he was waiting next to my car in the parking lot when I was ready to go home. I thought I'd be annoyed with his overprotectiveness, but as I drive to my apartment, I can't make the smile fall from my face.

When we're back at my place, Bentley greets me at the stairs. "Mind if I come in?"

"Only if you don't judge the mess," I say as I try to remember what things I failed to clean up most recently.

He grabs my hand and leads the way. "It wouldn't be yours if it wasn't messy."

"Hey." I attempt to shove him, but he's like a brick wall. "I take offense to that."

Bentley laughs. "Good. Maybe you'll start to clean more."

I consider sending him on his way, but I like when he's at my house. Makes him seem less... I don't know. Even though I don't outwardly show my feelings about how rich he is, it's nice when we're not reminded of it constantly.

Once we're inside, Bentley makes himself comfortable on my couch, and I head to the kitchen to grab take-out menus. I'm not much of a cook and I don't assume he'll want ramen or raviolis.

"Burgers, Chinese, or Italian? My treat," I say, dangling the options in front of his face from behind him.

He reaches back and grabs my hips, somehow pulling me over the couch. Before I can register what's happened, I'm on his lap.

I laugh. "That was impressive."

He raises a brow. "Did you expect anything less?"

I didn't, but I don't tell him that. "I mean, you lack in other areas, so it's good that you've got muscles to help compensate."

His fingers dig into my ribs, and I squirm, too ticklish for that kind of move.

Bentley realizes this too and takes advantage, sitting up and pinning me beneath him. "Let's see where else I can *compensate.*"

He lifts my shirt up, and his prickly face attacks my stomach while I squeal like a little schoolgirl. "I'm going to make you pay for this!"

His eyes peek up at me, and he smirks. "Yeah? How so?"

I nod to the box of toys that have sat untouched for weeks on top of my dresser. "With one of those."

I might have joked that he was kinky, but in reality, I've only seen a dominating side of Bentley, so when he stares at the box with a slight tilt of his head, seeming intrigued by the idea, I squirm out from underneath him.

My strides quicken and I grab the box, holding up a small pink vibrator, but he shakes his head. "You're not using that on me."

"Oh, come on. A little dildo never hurt anyone." I step closer, and he snatches it. The box ends up on the bed behind me.

"Let's prove that theory on you first."

Fuck yes, I think as I strip my work clothes off, letting them fly behind me, landing wherever they may.

Bentley shakes his head while unbuttoning his shirt. "No wonder your house is never clean."

By the time he's done—his clothes neatly draped over the couch—I'm lying in my bed with all my goodies next to me.

He stalks closer, and I drag the vibrator over my pussy. A moan slips from between my lips and Bentley's eyes go dark in an instant.

The dildo is no longer in my hands, and he's leaning over me. "If this is going inside you, I'm putting it there."

"By all means, the stage is yours." My chest is heaving. I'm needy as fuck for whatever it is he plans to do to me.

Bentley eyes the box first. His fingers dig through the items, likely finding lube, a couple more dildos and vibrators of varying sizes and colors, and a thing or two he might not recognize, like the clit-sucker the sales lady said I just had to have. Spoiler alert: she was right.

"Interesting choices you've got here," he murmurs, then spreads my legs and palms my pussy.

My hips buck beneath his touch. "A man isn't always needed for pleasure."

Bentley smirks. "He is if you want proper orgasms."

Before I can respond, the backs of my knees are settled over his shoulders and Bentley's mouth is attacking my clit, sucking hard and already driving me wild.

I dig my hands into his hair, grateful he keeps the strands a few inches long. My head tilts back and presses into the mattress when I arch my back, pushing closer to his face.

When my inner walls start to tighten around his newly added fingers, he pulls out, but I don't get the chance to complain.

Instead, that little pink vibrator makes a quick reappearance. Bentley glides it along my ass cheeks, then right into my pussy.

I release my hold on him and grip the bed as the world starts to fall out from under me. Holy fuck. I've used that dildo a dozen times, but it's never hit like that.

Shivers race down my spine and pool at my center, making me feel like I'm floating in water instead of lying on the bed.

Bentley glides the vibrator in and out of me, staring intently between my shaking thighs while I watch him, trying to get my wits back. His eyes finally meet mine, but I don't have the ability to form words.

Fucker knows it, too, because he smirks, pulls the vibrator out, and leans over me. "What next?"

I'm not sure I can handle anything else next, but Bentley seems to be having fun, so I don't dare object.

"What's this do?" he asks, holding up the clit-sucker.

I grin. "Something your mouth is better at."

He glances at it again, presses the on button, then puts the suction to his palm. His brows raise. "Interesting."

I wait with bated breath to see what he's going to do next. When he eyes the box again, I think I'm in the clear of using that particular toy, but then he smirks, and I know an idea has formed. One that could very well make me black out from pleasure.

Bentley shoves the box out of his way and positions himself over me, but it's not his face I'm seeing, it's his thick cock.

My hands wrap around the pulsing length and just as my lips form an O to suck him off, the clit-sucker starts doing its job.

"Mother freaking hell. I'd recommend giving a girl warning when your dick is at risk of getting chomped on," I say through gritted teeth.

He merely chuckles, then runs his tongue around the head of the toy, barely touching my pussy, but driving me wild anyway.

I loosen my grip on his cock and suck the tip into my mouth. He continues to assault me with his fingers, mouth, and that damn clit-sucker. I'm falling apart at the seams in all the best ways, but I want Bentley to come with me at the courtesy of one of my toys.

While he's distracted down south, I reach back and grab the first vibrator I find. It's a smaller one and perfect for what I have planned.

One of my hands sneaks around his waist, anchoring him in place while my mouth still sucks hard on his swelling dick. The other hand brings the vibrator to his balls, and I turn it on the lowest setting.

The black toy nestles right in, and he flinches so hard I nearly choke from the forward thrust of his cock.

"Kenzie," he warns, but I don't let up. Not when my legs are nearly numb and I'm ready to explode around his face just as soon as I can get him on the same page.

His hips move over my head, and I swirl my tongue around the thick head that's covered in precum. I move the vibrator around his balls slowly, then settle it right at the base of his cock before turning the setting up now that he's had a minute to get used to the sensation.

He tenses above me, and I continue dragging the pulsing tip between his balls and cock while my mouth devours the rest.

Then he changes the tide on me and turns up the clit-sucker. I cry out from the intensity. "Fuck me."

"That's next," he murmurs over my pussy.

I feel his balls tightening and take more of him into my mouth. The rest of my body is rocking with pulsing need, and we're both so close.

I drop the vibrator and squeeze his balls with one hand while I take him as deep as I can without gagging.

His mouth replaces the clit-sucker, and I lose all ability to hold out. My screams vibrate around his dick, and he stiffens inside my mouth. Cum shoots to the back of my throat and I barely swallow fast enough before my vision is faltering and I'm only seeing sporadic flickers of light in my vision.

Bentley rolls off me. Both of our chests are heaving, and

I can't move. My body is dead weight, and not even a fire could pry me out of bed.

This man has destroyed me in all the best ways.

"That was...more than interesting," he finally says.

I manage to chuckle. "That's one way to describe the best orgasm you've ever had."

"Maybe for you," he says cockily, but I don't believe him.

I'm going to have him hooked on toys in no time, and I'm going to ruin him for all others. One pleasurable moment at a time.

Chapter Twenty-Four

YOU'RE FIRED

Bentley

That Friday, Kenzie is having another girl's night and I'm stuck at work with Owen. I could go home, but since their house seems to be the place for the women to gather and he's been banished, I decide to stick around.

"Did you get the management on board at Sampson's for the pop art branding?" I ask from across the table.

We're in the conference room and among the last few still in the building. The extra room is helpful.

He nods. "Martha agreed it was just the kind of change that they needed. We're rolling out everything next month before people get too distracted with the holidays."

"Good call," I say, reorganizing the folder I've just finished going over. I look back up at him. "I'm meeting with the board on Wednesday next week."

He cocks his head. "Yeah? About anything in particular?"

I grin. He knows damn well what I'm going to talk to

them about. Owen officially gave me his interest in the Vice President position last week.

"Not much. Just maybe creating a new position within the company. Nothing serious," I reply and divert my eyes back to the papers in front of me.

I hear his pen drop onto the table. "You know, I really appreciate you giving me a chance at this opportunity. I know you can't guarantee anything, but to even be considered means a lot."

My stare meets his again. "You've worked for this company for over five years now. Hell, you put up with more than any sane person ever would. You deserve this. I know it, and so will the board if they don't already."

"Thanks, man. I'm glad that part of my life is over now. It's crazy how quickly things can change. Hell, I'd only known Ella a few days and I was ready to throw all of this away without blinking. You know what I mean?" Owen asks with a wistful smile on his face.

Fuck, do I.

But I've barely even admitted that to myself. I'm not about ready to do so with an employee. Though, that's more of an excuse. I've already accepted that Owen has quickly become a friend I can trust.

"Yeah, life has a way of shaking things up," I say, thinking about how Kenzie *shook* things up the other night with her little box of toys. My shoulders shudder just remembering what that vixen did to me with her little vibrator.

Owen laughs. "Oh, man. You've got it bad, and you don't even really know it, do you?"

My face scrunches. "Know what?"

He leans back in his chair. "I know I haven't really asked about you and Kenzie, but I know you didn't just stay late with me tonight because you had your own shit that couldn't wait until next week. I'm going to go out on a limb here and say it's because we're friends since that's how I think of you now. If you hadn't stayed with me, you knew I'd be here, sulking, all by myself."

I shrug. He's not wrong.

"Well, then. I feel like I can say I've been watching the changes in you around Kenzie, and I've seen the changes in her over the last month. The two of you, regardless of how different you are, work together. I assume you at least know that?"

"I do. I wouldn't be dating her if I didn't," I reply, suddenly intrigued by where he's going with this.

"You're not just dating Kenzie. You love her," Owen says so simply and matter-of-fact, but the moment he says the words, I feel like the ground has crumbled out from beneath me.

My chest tightens, breathing is nearly possible, and my mouth is drier than the Sahara.

Love? No, I didn't love Kenzie.

Sure, I enjoy ending my days with her in my bed. I like how she challenges me to not only relax, but to appreciate life more. She has a way of making me smile like nobody else does and...*fuck*.

Owen points at me, then smacks the tabletop. "There you go. I can't believe you didn't see it before."

Hell, neither can I.

I glare at him. "You tell Ella about this and you're fired."

He chuckles. "There are some things my soon-to-be wife doesn't need to know, and this is one of them. Bro code and all."

I've never had anyone I could have a bro code with. Maybe Kenzie storming into my life has made things better in more ways than I've really yet to consider.

My phone vibrates, and I anxiously flip it over, hoping to see Kenzie's name. Disappointment fills me when I see Celia's.

"Hey, sis," I answer the call.

"I still have over five hundred penises to make, and that fucking oven just blew another fuse!" She yells so loudly in my ear that I have to pull the phone away.

Owen's eyes widen, telling me he didn't miss the comment about the penises, either.

"Calm down. I'll run to the store and get a new box of fuses, then I can replace them all and you shouldn't have to worry about them." I gather my files together and get ready to leave.

She lets out a huge sigh. "Thank you, Bentley. I don't know what I'd do without you."

"You know you're going to have to figure out a way to mass produce these cookies outside of your shop if you keep selling this much, right?" I say, because the oven might have blown a fuse, but I'm pretty sure it's because of overuse, not a faulty piece of machinery.

"Yeah, yeah. I'll work on it after this weekend, but since I'm helping you tomorrow, I don't have time to worry about other solutions," she whines.

"Alright. See you soon." I end the call and glance at Owen. "I gotta go."

He grins. "So I gathered. Do you want help?"

My eyes widen ever so slightly. "Do you really want to get sweet-talked into helping make hundreds of penis cookies?"

He grimaces. "Not really."

"Didn't think so. Hopefully you can go home soon." I actually feel bad leaving him here by himself, which is an odd feeling.

He chuckles. "I doubt those women will be done with 'girls' night' anytime soon, but I might be able to sneak in and hide in the bedroom soon."

I frown as I wave goodbye and head for the door. Is that what I'm signing up for by letting Kenzie in all the way? Sneaking into my own house when she has friends over?

The answer is most likely, but surprisingly, I don't actually consider that a bad thing.

———

WITHIN THE LAST HOUR, I'VE GONE TO THE STORE for parts, picked up tacos for me and my sister, and changed all of the fuses out on the oven. Now, I'm ready to go home since we have a big day tomorrow for the carnival, but the tears welling in Celia's eyes aren't boding well for me.

"I don't know how I'm going to get all this done and get even a few hours of rest for tomorrow." Her palms rub over her face, and her shoulders shake.

"I can stay and help for a while. Kenzie's busy with her friends anyway," I say, almost a little regrettably. If I didn't need my sister to be present and reliable tomorrow, then I'd never agree to make dick cookies.

Celia pouts. "I know. They invited me, and I was so mad I couldn't join them." Then, she looks up at me with wide eyes. "You'll really help me?"

I wrap an arm around her. "I've got you, sis. Tell me what to do."

She brightens and goes around the table to grab containers of ingredients and tosses a measuring cup in each of them before placing an empty bowl in front of me. "One scoop of each of these goes into this one plus an egg and one of these butter sticks I've already measured. Once you have everything in, knead it all together, but not too rough. Be gentle with dough or it won't rise right. When you have a good enough consistency, throw some flour on the tabletop and you can finish kneading on the counter. I'll take over after that."

I already feel underqualified, and I haven't even started helping. "How many batches of these do I need to do in order for you to have the rest of the cookies you need?"

She bites her lower lip and stares at the floor. "Probably twenty? Maybe more if some batches don't pass quality checks."

Fuck. It's already eight. We can't do this on our own.

I pull out my phone and click on my messages. I feel bad interrupting Kenzie's night, but I have a feeling she'd be more pissed at me for not telling her Celia needed help.

Me: *Celia is in over her head. How do you feel about baking?*

Kenzie: *If it's dick cookies, count us in.*

I sigh and respond. ***I'll see you soon then.***

My eyes meet Celia's. "Kenzie, Ella, and Piper are coming to help. We'll get this done in no time."

She starts to cry, and I go around the counter to hug her again. "I don't know what I'd do without you," she mumbles against my chest.

I pat her back. "Good thing you never have to find out."

She nods and sniffles as I take a step back. Even if we have help coming, I still don't want to be here any longer than we have to be.

It's time to make dick cookies.

A phrase I hope I never have to think or say again.

Chapter Twenty-Five

RIGHT KIND OF DIFFERENT

Kenzie

I'VE GOT A DRINK IN MY HAND, MY BEST FRIENDS sitting on each side of me, and the flickering flames of Ella's firepit to further relax me as I lean back in the new zero-gravity chairs she and Owen just bought.

"I'm getting one of these as soon as I'm settled," Piper mutters.

I look over and her eyes are closed. Her wine glass is barely being held up by two of her fingers.

"Easy there, Pipe. You don't want to be the crazy neighbor who sleeps outside after enjoying her evening a little too much," I joke.

Ella leans forward. "Speaking of neighbors. Have you gotten the information for your new place yet now that a date is finalized?"

Piper nods. "Just got it yesterday, actually, but I've been so busy, I kinda pushed thoughts of moving to the back of my mind." She pulls out her phone, clicks a few buttons, then hands it to me. "Take a look."

I position the phone between me and Ella. The first picture is of a row of six townhouses. Each one is a different color, but they all have wooden shutters, a white front door, and a perfectly manicured yard. In the next one is a picture of a sage green house.

"Is this one yours?" I ask Piper before continuing, and she nods.

Ella leans in closer. "Is this temporary, or do you get to rent it for however long you want?"

"I can rent for up to twelve months, and then I'll have the option of moving or buying the house." There's a sadness in her voice that we're all feeling.

This might be the opportunity Piper has worked her ass off for, but that doesn't mean the idea of her putting real roots down in LA and buying her first home doesn't feel all kinds of wrong.

Ella points at the phone. "A pool? Hell, yes. I can't wait to visit and use it."

That brightens Piper's mood some at least.

I know we'll visit as much as we both can, but it still won't be the same or enough.

We finish scanning the pictures and I hand the phone to Piper. "It's going to be perfect for you." I offer a wide smile. "And the guest room will need bunk beds. I'm not sleeping on the same mattress as Ella. I don't know how Owen handles her tossing and turning."

Ella laughs. "He does a better job of tiring me out. My sleep is much more sound these days."

I give her a high five. "That's my girl. Now, speaking of you and Owen. Did you lock in a venue yet?"

Piper and I have been going stir crazy not being able to start planning the wedding for them. I'm more than ready to see my best friend walk down the aisle toward the man that was made perfectly for her.

She grins widely and nods. "I was going to tell you guys when Owen was around, but since you asked... We found out this week that the rustic barn spot had a cancellation for December, and we are locked in for the third."

All three of us squeal in unison.

That is, until Piper starts crying.

I reach for her. "Hey, what's with the waterworks?"

"I might have missed the wedding." Piper wipes furiously at her cheeks. "What else am I going to miss?"

Ella is up and out of her chair at the same time I am. We wrap our arms around our friend and hold her tight.

"You're going to miss little things," Ella starts, sniffling a little herself, "but we promise to make sure you're here for all of the big stuff. Even Owen agreed that we had to take that date even though it was sooner than we originally planned. We didn't want to chance anything else conflicting with your schedule once you're gone."

Piper hiccups so hard that I'm afraid she's going to break something. I grab on to her shoulder and squeeze tight, looking right into her red-rimmed eyes. "Hey, everything is going to be okay. You're probably going to be grateful for a break from my crazy."

She snorts and wipes at her face again. "I secretly love your crazy and you know it."

I grin. "Of course I do, but that's not the point. The point I'm trying to make is that you're going to be okay. You're going to be a kick-ass editor, move your way up to whatever comes next, sign the next big-name author, meet all the celebrities who you'll tell wild stories to about your friends all the way in North Carolina. Some might even find us interesting enough to want to do a TV show about us. I mean, Ella and Owen's story would make for some epic rom-com shit on screen."

Ella gives me a little shove. "Says the person who's dating a billionaire."

I smirk. "Dating, fucking. I guess the two can go hand-in-hand."

Piper rolls her eyes. "Don't pretend you're not head over heels for Bentley. We've never seen you like this with any other guy."

"Like what?" I ask, almost nervously.

Piper taps her chin. "Oh, I don't know. How about how blissed you've been for weeks and you're not continually smiling because you know you're hilarious, but because you're truly happy with life and the work you're doing and the people in it. Or what about all the times you've slept over at Bentley's house these last couple months and how many times you've had him at yours. A place where no man ever has stayed a full night until Bentley."

Okay, she has a point, but I'm just not there yet. My heart has only been cracked open twice. It's not often I let someone in far enough to make a dent in my feelings. While I think Bentley is the right kind of different, I'm still hesitant to admit big emotions for him.

"Point made, my friend," I say before going back to my chair and grabbing my wine glass from the cupholder.

Ella shakes her head and grins at Piper. "She really *is* gonzo over Bentley. I've never seen her speechless."

I scoff. "I am not. I'm just parched."

I finish off my wine and before I can refill my glass, my phone pings with a text.

My Fucker: Celia is in over her head. How do you feel about baking?

Me: If it's dick cookies, count us in.

My Fucker: I'll see you soon then.

Piper and Ella are staring at me when I realize I'm grinning too big to be normal. Instead of addressing what I know they're thinking, I change the subject.

"Are either of you down to help Celia make dick cookies before we call it a night?" I ask.

Piper laughs. "Absolutely, but I'd help even if it wasn't dick cookies."

Of course she would. That's why we love her.

———

WITHIN THIRTY MINUTES, WE'RE INSIDE CELIA'S adorable bakery and prepped for work with freshly washed hands, hair covered with tacky nets, and matching pink aprons covering our fronts. The best part, though?

Bentley is wearing the same as all of us women.

Yes, my big, sexy man is donning a pink apron and looking seriously hot.

Celia claps her hands excitedly. "Okay, everyone knows what they're supposed to be doing. I'll be bouncing between each of you in case you have questions while also rotating cookies in and out of the oven. With any luck, we'll be out of here in a few hours."

She cringes, and I know she feels bad since we all need to be up early tomorrow, but it's not that big of a deal. At least, not for me.

I throw an arm around her. "Don't stress so much. We have Sunday to sleep in."

Celia's head shakes. "You might, but I'll be here baking for the storefront and packing all of these cookies shipments." Then, she groans. "Shit, I need more help. Who knew dicks could cause so many problems?"

Ella, Piper, and I all raise our hands at the same time, and laughter fills the room.

Well, at least from everyone without a dick. Bentley, however, is already back to work, kneading dough like a champ.

Things quiet down, and everyone goes back to their workstations, eager to get all the things done so we're not zombies tomorrow for the big event.

Celia joins me, inspecting my work. "It feels really wrong to compliment your penis-decorating skills when you're dating my brother, so I'm not going to, okay?"

I snort-laugh. "Understandable."

She sorts through the cooling cookies, tosses two aside, and throws one away. "I'm really thankful you and your friends came to help. I don't know what I was thinking when I failed to set a cap on orders. That's a mistake I won't make again."

I bite my lip, concentrating hard on the white piping

before I respond. "Do you have a website that will do all of that for you?"

"Sorta." She shrugs. "I can adjust things, but I also know it could be better. I've just been overwhelmed with the requests that I keep forgetting about all the other things that would probably make my life easier, but that I also don't have time to work on."

I nod. "I get that, but that's why you need to hire people to do things you no longer have time for."

"Funny. That's not the first time I've heard that today." Her face glows as she says the words and I'm intrigued.

"Oh, yeah? Who is the other genius in your life?" I ask innocently.

Celia glances back at her brother and finds him covered in flour and not paying attention to us. "Well, he's someone I hired to do some marketing things for me, but has also asked me out on a couple of dates. One of which I might have said yes to this week."

I grin and keep my voice calm. "Are you going to tell Bentley about him?"

"I kinda already did, but I hadn't gone on a date with the guy yet. I'll give it another date or two before I decide, but from how last night went..." Her cheeks flush. "I'd imagine they'll go well."

I nudge her with my elbow. "Good for you. Your secret is safe with me for now. Unless Bentley outright asks me, but the likelihood of that isn't high."

Celia laughs softly. "I don't imagine my brother likes to ask questions about my sex life."

"No, I bet not." I pick up the piping again while my smile still spreads from ear to ear.

I glance around the room before resuming decorating and let out a happy sigh. I could have never predicted my life would go from mundane and sexually frustrated to lively and satiated within a matter of months, but ever since the day of my promotion, things have only been looking up.

A lot is because of my hard work, and a little is because of the man across the room. My eyes find Bentley, and I watch the corded muscles in his forearms flex and loosen while he handles the dough like he's been baking his whole life.

His sleeves are rolled up to his elbows, and he's wearing that sexy pink apron, but he's still filthy. Thoughts of taking him to "clean up" consume my mind. At least, they do until he finally feels me staring and looks up.

Our gazes lock, and my heart slows while my chest expands.

My grumpy businessman. He's more like a firm teddy bear with a soft center and perfect blue eyes and a sexy five-o-clock shadow and full lips and rippling muscles and a dick that's to die for and...

"What the fuck?" I sputter and swipe at my face until I can see again.

Flour is everywhere, and I'm the only one in the room not laughing.

Piper leans in closer. "Next time, don't eye fuck your boyfriend when you're supposed to be working like the rest of us and you won't get anything thrown in your face."

Her sweetly spoken words are accompanied by an even sweeter smile that only Piper is capable of, but she hasn't embarrassed me.

I grab one of the cookies Celia set aside and swirl my tongue over the tip. "Would you rather I be more direct in my desires?"

Piper's smile fades away, and she gags, turning her attention back to the counter. "Never mind. Keep doing whatever you want."

I walk over to her and throw an arm around her shoulders. "I'm proud of you for trying to call me out, though. Next time, don't let it be about anything sexual and you just might catch me off guard."

"I think I'll just focus on what I'm supposed to be doing and go home before you," she mutters.

Girl has a point. If I want to fuck Bentley in the shower later, we better start moving our asses, or I'll be dead on my feet before we make it back to his place.

Chapter Twenty-Six

Bentley

My weary eyes glance at the clock when Kenzie and I stumble into my bedroom. Two-in-the-fucking-morning. My sister is lucky I love her. We're supposed to be well-rested for tomorrow—today, really—yet I haven't heard Kenzie form a coherent sentence since midnight.

Drinking with her friends and then doing manual labor equals a zombie Kenzie, but she's rather adorable so I haven't complained. Not even when I had to carry her up the stairs.

"Come on, gorgeous. We need to clean up or we'll be hating life even more when the sun comes up."

Maybe she wouldn't, but I would. Sleeping in filth isn't my idea of a good night's rest.

She mutters something I can't understand, then leans harder against my side.

I grip her hip tighter to keep her standing as I turn on

the shower and try to figure out how to get the both of us naked without laying Kenzie on the ground.

I hold her shoulders and give her a slight shake. "Kenzie. I need you awake for five more minutes. That's it."

Her eyes flutter, and she blinks several times before nodding.

"Can you stand here long enough to get undressed?" I ask.

"Yea-nope."

She sways, but I catch her and turn her around, positioning her hands on the towel rack. "Hold on to this. Really good for me."

Her forehead rests against the glass shower, and she seems to be balancing well enough, so I quickly strip out of my now white-dusted clothes, thanks to all the flour I handled.

As soon as I'm done, I unzip Kenzie's dress, thankful there aren't more clothes to remove from her body.

"Ti-werd," she whispers against my chest when I guide her under the warm water.

I brush her hair out of her face before turning us sideways. "I know. Almost done."

I don't bother with soap and opt for just rinsing both of us off.

By the time I'm done, Kenzie can't keep her eyes open anymore. I've never seen someone so exhausted in my life. I'm actually impressed with her right now. Slightly annoyed but impressed, nonetheless.

It's a struggle to get her dried off enough, but I manage it better once I settle her on the mattress instead of trying to do so standing up.

When we're both as ready for bed as we can get, I situate Kenzie onto the pillow, and she burrows in as I lay the comforter over her naked body.

Before I head to my side of the bed, I kiss the top of Kenzie's head, soaking in the shared electricity between the two of us.

Talking with Owen earlier and realizing that I don't just like Kenzie, but that I love this crazy woman, was an awakening I didn't expect.

I see her in a different light now. How caring she is for the people she allows into her life, how hard she tries in everything she does, how no matter how much snark spews from her full lips, she has a heart as big as all the oceans.

I also take in how perfect her round nose is, how the part in her hair always curves to the left at the back, and how her creamy skin glows under the moonlight coming through the bedroom window.

Fuck, how did I not see this before?

I mean, I had, just not all together. The longer I stare, the more I want to wake her up and show her my true feelings.

Except I know that's not going to happen. Not tonight anyway.

Instead, I settle for crawling into bed, holding Kenzie tightly against my chest, and falling asleep to the steady thrum of her heartbeat.

———

THE MORNING SET-UP WENT ABOUT HOW I expected: quiet with lots of caffeine being handed out to the volunteers.

With only a few minutes to spare, we finish getting all of the cats and dogs positioned around the booths, make sure everyone has enough supplies to last through the first wave of guests, and double-check that the vendors have all arrived.

So far, the worst thing to happen was a dog peeing in his crate, but that was easy to clean up. At least, it looked easy when I watched Sam take care of the mess.

I've hardly seen Kenzie this morning, but as I'm making my way over to the dunk tank, I spot her fiery red hair.

She's laughing with my sister whose face painting booth is only a few yards away. Kenzie is tossing a ball in her hand, and there's a glint in her eyes when they meet mine.

"What's going on?" I ask before leaning in to give her a quick kiss.

She pats my shoulder. "You're first up for the dunk tank since you arrived last."

I shake my head. "No, I was supposed to be collecting tickets for this booth, not participating in it."

"Well, plans changed. I need you in the hot seat, Bentley," Joyce's voice says from behind me.

I turn around and she's walking one of our newer puppies on a leash. "I didn't bring any extra clothes."

My excuse won't work with Joyce. I already know that, but I have to try.

She smiles widely. "We have donated clothes inside for volunteers when mishaps occur during their shifts. I'm sure you can find something to wear from that box if you get wet. Just remember, it's mostly kids. I'm sure they'll miss."

Kenzie is still tossing the ball in her palm, and I have a feeling I'll be soaked all too soon.

Instead of trying to talk my way out of it, I kick my tennis shoes off, empty my pockets, and grin as if this was my idea all along.

I climb into the tank, grateful the water isn't freezing, and take a seat on the wobbling board, *then* my stomach sinks.

Maybe I should have tried a little harder to get out of this.

"Oh, Bentley. Did I ever tell you what I spent my high school years doing?" Kenzie calls out, standing a good distance from the tank.

I cock my head to the side and don't respond when her grin widens.

"Fast-pitch softball."

A second later, she launches the ball toward the target and a bell goes off as the world falls out from under me.

Okay, maybe not the world, but I didn't actually expect her to hit the damn thing on the first try.

I spit and sputter and find my footing, then point at her with a glare on my face. "Not cool."

Her eyes roam my soaked chest. "Seems rather refreshing."

Celia laughs and gives Kenzie a high-five. "If you ever get tired of him, please don't think we're a package deal and ditch me too."

Kenzie throws her head back and says something I

don't catch as I get distracted by the rise and fall of her chest.

Once I'm back in my spot, my balls are freezing, but the sound of squeals and laughter around the one-acre property take over my attention.

There are tents, streamers, pet playpens, and the smell of popcorn wafting through the air. Of course, I'm always happy to see this event be a success, but since I've been more involved this time around, there's an extra sense of accomplishment as I watch kids begin to line up for the booths.

Kenzie has her back to me, collecting payment from parents and handing out baseballs to the kids. At least, I think they're all kids until I see Owen standing at the back. Word spread fast. Great.

Though, being back in the water right now sounds ideal. Sitting here wet, waiting to get dunked, isn't all it's cracked up to be.

By the time Owen gets to the front, I've only been in once more and I hope he's got his throwing arm ready.

"How's it going, Bentley?" he asks with a laugh.

I rock back and forth on the board. "Oh, you know. Just grand."

He smirks. "Uh huh."

Owen throws the ball and misses. Disappointment has never filled me so fast.

Though, he's too prideful to walk away and I'm in the water on the next throw. I purposely dunk my head and my shoulders shake. Fuck, I better not be in here all day.

———

THANKFULLY, THAT ISN'T THE CASE. AFTER dozens of kids send me into the water and I feel like a prune, I'm finally relieved of dunk tank duty. Even better, Kenzie convinced my assistant Brad to bring me the spare set of clothes I keep at the office for nights I'm running late to anything that I don't want to wear a suit to.

He hands me the bag once I've dried off as best I can with a towel, and he says, "It's good to see you so relaxed. I'm not used to it."

He's not supposed to be, but I don't tell him that. Not when he's just done me a huge favor. "Thanks for doing this. Are you going to stick around?"

Brad glances back at the row of cat crates. "Yeah, I think I just might."

Interesting. I didn't peg him for a cat person, but I at least know he'll be able to afford taking care of one of them.

I glance back at the poor sucker who took my place. I think Kenzie called him Glen, and she seems all too pleased that he's next up.

At least we're both happier being done with the dunk tank.

Though, as Joyce heads for us, I'm not sure whatever comes next will be any better.

Chapter Twenty-Seven

CUTS ME TO THE CORE

Kenzie

Caffeine becomes my life blood as the day goes on, but the more I drink, the less effective it becomes. Once Bentley was relieved of dunk tank duty, we tried to stick together, but there has been so much to do that it wasn't really possible.

Joyce finds me and grins excitedly. "Thank you again for everything you've done today. I'm so glad Joslin sent you to me."

"I am, too," I say earnestly, for more than one reason.

Joyce glances around. "Where's Bentley?"

"Last I saw, he was cleaning a litter box. Something I absolutely took a picture of." I plan on getting that one printed and hanging it on my wall.

She laughs and pulls me into a hug I don't expect. "I'm so glad the two of you finally started getting along. I was worried I was wrong about pairing the two of you together."

I start to question her but hear my name being called. I turn to find Louise, the little old lady from the bar, walking toward me.

Joyce pushes me toward her. "Go say hi, then find Bentley. The two of you are officially off duty for the night. I'll see you tomorrow for clean up."

A sigh of relief escapes me. "Thanks, Joyce." Then, I turn to greet Louise and realize she's holding a leash with a long-haired black dog at the end. "Find yourself a new companion?" I ask with a grin.

She nods excitedly. "Thought this was better than revisiting the bar. Hopefully you've had good luck there, though. Or at least snapped some pictures like I told you to."

I chuckle and lean in closer. "I actually ended up with the businessman."

"No shit? I'm impressed. Not that you're not good enough, but that you approached him after waiting so long. Good for you." The dog barks, making us both laugh. "Even Scooter agrees," she adds.

"Well, I can sleep a little better now that I have Scooter's approval." I lean down and scratch the dog's head.

Louise waggles her brows when I look back up. "Hopefully, you're sleeping less. At least you should be if you're doing things right." Before I can respond, she adds, "It's time for us to head home. Hopefully we'll see you around, Kenzie."

"I hope so, too," I say with a genuine smile, then watch them walk off toward the parking lot.

Now, I just need to find my boyfriend and get the hell home before I fall over on my feet and sleep in the grass.

I head toward Celia first and find her still painting faces, but thankfully, she looks like she's on her last one.

"Hey, have you seen your brother?" I ask when I approach.

She keeps her eyes on the woman's face while she answers. "No, but I could really use some new water to clean all my brushes when I'm done with this one if you're not busy."

Her voice is groggy, and I know she's just as tired as I am, if not more.

"I'll go grab some from the tent. Be right back."

She nods, staying focused, and I go off to retrieve some water bottles for her. My eyes scan for Bentley, but I still don't see him. I'll have to give him a call once I'm done helping Celia if he doesn't appear before then.

Just as I step under the tent, I hear a woman's voice.

"Excuse me? Are you a volunteer here?" she asks.

I turn around and nod. "How can I help you?"

"I'm doing a story about the event. I was hoping to ask you a few questions if you have a minute," she says.

I want to say yes, but when I look into her amber eyes, take in the skirt and heels that don't fit in here, something seems off. Plus, from what I knew, all of the reporters left when the sun started setting and most of the pets had been adopted.

"Please? I got here late, and my boss will kill me if I don't find someone to help with the article." She brushes strands of ebony hair behind her ear and begs me with her round eyes.

Shit. How am I supposed to say no to that? "Sure. What questions do you have?"

She perks up quickly and pulls out a recorder. I want to ask why she needs that, but my exhaustion is setting further in. Instead of prolonging the inevitable, I lean against the table behind me and use it to help keep me on my feet.

"How long have you been a volunteer for Resolutions?" she asks first.

"Only a couple months, but it's been a great experience so far. The owner Joyce really cares for all of these animals," I say.

What seems like a forced smile rises on her face. "Great. What about the other volunteers? Do you work closely with them?"

That's a weird fucking question, so I shrug. "When necessary."

"I see. What about Bentley Abbott? I hear he's a big contributor to the shelter." Her tone is tightening and I'm not liking the direction of this conversation. The thought occurs to me that this one might not be a local reporter. She very well could be from that damned online magazine.

Damn it. They just couldn't leave well enough alone. Well, maybe I could make Bentley sound like the least interesting person ever and they'll finally leave him alone.

"He's on the board. Pretty quiet and only focuses on his work. Donates money when needed. Nothing exciting there," I say, meeting her stare while keeping my face neutral.

Her lips thin and she grips the recorder tighter. "I see. So, you don't interact with him often?"

"Not really," I answer then yawn. "I really should be going."

She pulls a pen and paper from her pocket. "Would you

mind writing your information down for me in case I have any follow up questions?"

I want to tell her to fuck off, but instead, I accept the offered items and turn toward the table to write down fake information.

As I'm making up a phone number, she continues with her questions. "Are you sure there's nothing between you and Bentley? I swear I saw the two of you together before."

I hold in the profanity and words I really want to sling at the intrusive woman and lie again.

"Maybe, but Bentley's nothing to me. I prefer my men more rugged, if you know what I mean?" I let out a nervous laugh. I really should have thought through my responses better, but I'm so fucking tired and I just want her to leave me alone.

"Interesting. I don't actually know what you mean," the reporter replies, still holding her recorder out. It seems even closer to me than before.

I hand the paper back to her. "I mean, don't get me wrong, he's nice on the eyes, but he's not my kind of boyfriend material or anything noteworthy. Just another suit with a big bank account. I really only got to know him because of this event."

Oh, God. Now, I'm just blabbering nonsense, and this causes the woman to smile, which makes me want to punch her in the face.

I'm one second from telling her to fuck off when I hear Bentley start to speak.

"Glad to know what you actually think of me, McKenzie." His chest is heaving and hands are balled into fists at his sides as he sneers at me.

I open my mouth to say anything that will fix this fucked situation, but he swivels around to leave before I can.

Forgetting about the reporter, I jog to catch up to him and snag his wrist to stop his forward movements. "That wasn't what it sounded like. She's a—"

His eyes narrow and darken when he finally glances at me. His head lowers, and his voice is menacing. "I don't give a single fuck who that woman is. I only cared who you were, and clearly, I was wrong about who I thought that was. Now, you can go fuck yourself and leave me alone."

Shock cuts me to the core, and tears well in my eyes. He can't be serious. Hell, this can't be happening.

By the time I'm capable of functioning again, I shove my tears down and turn back to the reporter to take my aggressions out on her, but she's gone. Then, I see Celia heading my way with a confused look on her face.

"What's going on? Why was Bentley storming off?" she asks quickly.

I put my head in my hands and mutter, "Everything just went really wrong, really fucking quickly."

She grabs my elbows and tugs on them until I look at her. "Where is Bentley going?"

A few tears slip down my cheeks. "Home, probably. He left after hearing something that I said, but didn't mean."

Celia guides me to a bench under the tent. "Tell me everything."

"There was a reporter who started asking me questions when I came to get a few waters for you. I got suspicious of her when she quickly started asking about Bentley, and I panicked thinking she wasn't just one of the locals, but someone from that online magazine. I lied to her, trying to make Bentley sound uninteresting, in hopes she would go away, but before she could, Bentley showed up and heard me possibly saying he was nothing more than a suit with a big bank account."

Repeating my early words now, it truly sets in how fucked up they were, even if I was trying to keep my and Bentley's personal information out of that reporter's mouth. In my defense, my lack of sleep and the nerves that slammed into me when I thought I was talking to a paparazzi-type reporter made me panic. I felt cornered and just wanted her to go away. Though, that sounds like a pathetic excuse even to me.

Celia rubs her hand over my back. "It's okay. Once you explain, I'm sure Bentley will understand."

My head shakes. "I don't think he will. You didn't see the look in his eyes, Celia. He hated me in that moment."

She offers me a small smile. "You can't really hate someone without loving them first. Just give him some time to cool off and you can explain."

I want to believe she's right, but every time I close my eyes, all I see is the hurt on Bentley's face.

His money is his least favorite thing about himself, and I'd chosen the exact wrong words to use. Fuck, that was so stupid. I should have just pushed that woman out of my way when she kept on with the questions. I should have told her to kiss my ass. I should have just kept my damn mouth shut instead of thinking I could outsmart a reporter.

I glance around the carnival, trying to find that woman so I can tell her what I really think about her questions, but she's nowhere to be found.

"If I ever see that dark-haired bitch and her ridiculous heels again, she'll never forget meeting me," I say to Celia as I swipe at my cheeks again.

Everything in my chest aches, and I don't know how I'm going to survive the night without setting things right with Bentley.

"I should go to his house, right? He'll have to go home eventually," I say to Celia, but she's not looking at me.

"You said the reporter had dark hair and was wearing heels? What else?" Celia asks, eyes continuing to search the crowd.

I'm confused on why she's asking but indulge her anyway. "Umm, a black shirt and red button up top. Why?"

Celia turns back to me and grabs my hand tightly. "That wasn't a reporter, Kenzie."

My head is swirling with confusion. "Yes, she was. She had a recorder and pen and paper... Okay, that was it, but still. She said she was and looked the part."

"I think it was Selene. Did Bentley tell you about her?" Celia bites her bottom lip.

Her sudden nerves make my stomach roll. "No. Who is that?"

"She's my friend. Or she was, until this moment. I hooked her up with Bentley, but she wasn't what he wanted, and they broke up for the final time before he went to Peru this summer. She's wanted him back ever since he returned, but I brushed her off, thinking she was harmless. I swore I saw her earlier, but I was so busy I couldn't be sure. I think she was trying to set you up. I told her the paparazzi were looking into us. I thought I could trust her still, especially when it seemed like she was backing off my brother."

My chest feels empty. "Bentley was going to hear what I said even if he hadn't come to find me."

Celia nods. "If you said she had a recorder, I have no doubt. Sounds like she was goading you into saying exactly what she knew Bentley wouldn't want to hear."

"That fucking bitch." I'm seething, and I want to beat the hell out of a woman I don't even know.

Celia grabs my hand. "Let me handle Selene. I know where to hurt her the most. I might not live for the higher society lifestyle like she does, but I still know plenty of people."

"I'd rather give her a couple black eyes and a broken nose," I growl.

She laughs. "I know, but that would only garner her more sympathy. Something she doesn't deserve and is rather good at getting. I only wish I'd seen her true colors sooner."

I meet Celia's blue eyes. Seeing them reminds me of Bentley and only makes my heart shatter more. "I can't lose him."

Her arm wraps around me. "And you're not going to. I'm going to help you make this right, but first, tell me what you need."

"Ella and Piper would help. They've been supervising the ring toss all day." Celia has been great, but I need my two best friends as well. I need their hugs and love and words.

Celia nods in that direction. "Go find them, then I'll tell Joyce we're all leaving. I doubt she'll mind since most of the guests are gone and takedown isn't until tomorrow, anyway."

I nod and get up almost robotically. Everything in me feels dead until I picture Selene's smug face, then I'm back to murderous and the rapidly changing emotions are taking everything out of me.

When I find Ella and Piper, they're already wrapping up and laughing as they pick rings from the barrels. That is only until they see me.

Ella tenses, clinging to a ring between her hands. "What happened?"

"I don't even know. Too much to explain here, but Bentley left and I'm not okay." I barely get the words out before new tears fall.

I've never been the kind of woman to cry over a man. Yet, there I was, with nothing snarky to say and feeling lower than I have in years.

Piper reaches me first and wraps her arms around me. "Whatever happened, I'm sure it can be fixed."

I snort. "Only if he'll listen to me."

Ella joins. "We'll tie him to a chair if we have to."

I let them hold me for a few minutes before I straighten. "I won't beg him. He'll either listen, or he won't. If he cares about me, then I shouldn't have to plead for time to explain."

Ella brushes hair out of my face. "While that's true, love makes people do crazy things when they're hurt. Whatever happened, it might not be allowing Bentley to act rationally and you're going to have to bend a little, too, even if you don't think you did anything wrong."

She's right and I know it, but the more time that passes,

the less okay I am with how Bentley stormed off. Yes, I said something hurtful, but he didn't have to be a child about it. He should have let me explain instead of telling me to go fuck myself.

I run a hand through my hair. "Damn it, this is stupid."

Piper leans closer to me. "Nothing good in life comes easy. We've all learned that a time or two, don't you agree?"

I pout and lean harder against her. "I don't want to agree."

She smiles. "Nobody ever does when it's their turn to fight for what they want. Come on. Tell us what happened, and we'll help fix it."

Fuck, I hope they can.

Chapter Twenty-Eight

KNOW THE TRUTH

Bentley

It's been two days since the night at the carnival, and I still can't calm my racing heart. Not even spending the last thirty-six hours in the office has helped distract me. I'd only gone home long enough to grab some clothes, because I knew at least Celia would come looking for me. Then, I decided to spend the last two nights at work. Dramatic? Possibly, but it was the only safe place I knew I could be while I attempted to sort my thoughts.

I thought Kenzie was different, but hearing her say that I meant nothing to her and I was nothing more than a suit with a big bank account... That cut deep. More than I would have expected.

Of course, admitting to Owen that I loved her the night before the fundraiser didn't help matters.

I never should have let her in. Never should have fallen victim to her loud mouth and—no. I can't think about why I fell for her. I just need to move the fuck on.

When I get back to my office after using the gym and shower at work, I spot Owen sitting in front of my desk.

He's among the few people I don't want to see right now. That's maybe not fair to him since I felt like we'd become friends, but I just can't handle him defending *her*. Not right now.

"Owen, I'm not doing this here," I say with conviction.

He turns around in his seat, his eyes following my movements. "Is that so? Well, from the looks of it in here and the many emails I saw sent out yesterday, you've been in the office working since you left the carnival. I would take that to mean that you actually have some free time on your hands, and I'm not going anywhere until you listen to me."

I cross my arms and lift a brow. "Is that so?"

"Hear me out, Bentley. Not too long ago, Kenzie did that for me and the choice she made is possibly the only reason I'm planning a wedding to the woman of my dreams. If you care about her as much as I think you do, then you need to know what I do. If that still doesn't change anything for you, at least nobody will be left with what ifs."

Owen's words are resolute, but I don't want to hear about Kenzie from someone else. Especially not when she hasn't even left me a voicemail or sent a text. Sure, she called a few times that first night, but her silence speaks volumes about what I heard.

"Kenzie doesn't give a shit about me. I don't know why you're defending her when she hasn't even done so herself," I say and lean back in my chair with a huff.

Owen chuckles softly. "God, the two of you are so stubborn. Kenzie refuses to give you the truth if you refuse to speak to her. So, if you won't do that, then I'll tell you what happened. And if you don't want to listen to me, your sister will be here after she's done baking this morning, but I figured you'd rather hear from me."

My fingers drum over my forearms. I don't want to hear from either of them, but if Owen is putting his ass on the line like this, maybe he can tell me something that will help lessen the amount of rage I still have pumping through my veins.

"What do you want to tell me?" I ask with a clipped tone.

He leans forward. "Did you see the woman Kenzie was talking to?"

I shake my head. "I was too pissed off to take in much else around me."

"That's what I figured." Owen sighs. "She was talking to a woman who said she was a reporter. Had a voice recorder and seemed legit. When she started asking direct questions about you, Kenzie freaked out, thanks to the recent stuff with the paparazzi, and overcompensated. She thought she was protecting you by not divulging your relationship with her."

While I can see the truth in what Owen is saying, it doesn't change anything for me.

"Kenzie should have walked away. Instead, she insulted me. That's not what I call protective," I say.

Owen nods. "You're right, but Kenzie was set up to fail the moment she answered that woman's first question. Do you want to know who the reporter was? Don't bother guessing. It was your ex Selene. She was setting Kenzie up. At least that's what Celia told Ella. Selene wanted Kenzie to slip up so that she could share the recording with you, but she lucked out. You showed up to hear the words for yourself."

Pain pierces my chest. "No."

"Actually, yes. Celia showed Kenzie a picture of Selene and confirmed what they already believed to be true. Selene set out to ruin your new relationship, and she succeeded. Are you going to let that last?" Owen asks with a challenge in his voice.

Fuck. Am I? I don't know. I want to say his words change things, but Kenzie still said what she said instead of just walking away. How am I supposed to trust her if she does shit like that?

Owen stands. "I won't bring this up again. You're still my boss, and I respect you no matter how the rest of this plays out, but I also care about Kenzie, and you need to know the truth."

I offer him a stiff nod. "Thanks."

Owen sees himself out, and I'm left sitting in my desk chair, more confused than I've ever been in my entire life.

What the fuck am I going to do now?

Chapter Twenty-Nine

THE SUN TO MY STORM

Kenzie

WORK PASSES TORTUROUSLY SLOW. NOT TEXTING
or calling Bentley has been killing me, but I won't beg him
to hear me out. I refuse. Him being such a child about this
whole situation is showing me a side of Bentley I didn't
think existed, so I'm glad it happened now.

I was falling hard for him. Hell, I'm pretty sure I love
him, but that kind of emotion isn't just swept to the side
when things get hard. No, if Bentley cared about me as
much as I do for him, he wouldn't have ignored me. Not
like this.

Though, Piper's previous words are still taunting me.
"But if love isn't just swept to the side, why have you given
up already? He shouldn't have to be the only one to fight."

Yes, she's right, but at least I tried at first. Bentley simply
walked the fuck away.

I check my phone one last time before I head to my car.
It's time to go home. To my empty apartment. By myself.

Damn it. I didn't realize how much I was beginning to despise my way of living until now.

There are no new messages from Bentley. Only a few from Piper and Ella and one from Celia inviting me over to her place.

As much as I adore her, I don't think I can hang with her anymore. At least not until I'm certain the possibility of seeing Bentley won't make me want to throw things at his stupidly perfect face.

I make my way to my car and head home. Maybe I can spend the night looking at real estate. I could distract myself with thoughts of moving and pretending I was already living in another person's house.

Yeah, that will help. I'll order Chinese. Nothing makes things better like fried rice.

With my evening sorted, I manage to get through the rush of traffic in one piece, but when I think safety is within my reach, I see an all-too-familiar black SUV in the parking lot of my apartment complex.

I park and sit in the driver's seat. I wanted to see Bentley before, but now? I don't know. I'm not ready for him to rip my heart out again. I'm not ready for him to tell me he doesn't believe I said those things to protect him. Sure, it was a dumb attempt—I realize that now—but my intentions were good.

A few minutes later, I grab my purse and get out of my car. When I peek inside his Range Rover, it's empty. I try to steel my heart for seeing his face, but every step up the stairs gets heavier.

I want to turn tail and go anywhere but home. Except I

also don't want to drag this out. I just want to be done with this whole awful situation.

Okay, that's a lie. Bentley isn't just a situation, and our time together wasn't awful, but still... I'm ready to move forward in my life. Not to wallow in heartbreak.

Bentley is leaning against my door when I get to the landing. He's dressed in a fresh blue button-up and gray slacks. His hands are loose at his sides, and everything about his body is relaxed until I meet his eyes.

The icy blues are brighter than normal and stare daggers into my soul.

Shit, I'm not ready to face him after more than a day of radio silence.

He steps forward, but I hold my hand out. "I can't do this, Bentley. I could have thrown down with you at the carnival. Hell, I would have gone rounds even yesterday, but not today. Tonight, I need to be on my own."

He takes a step closer. "And what about tomorrow night?"

"I don't know," I answer honestly.

Bentley's hand lifts and lowers. "I don't like seeing the fire gone from your eyes."

I scoff. "Then, maybe you shouldn't have walked away from me."

"You called me a suit and bank account. What did you think I was going to do? If I'd stayed, I'd have said things I couldn't take back, and a part of me, even after what I heard, still believed you deserved better than that."

My arms cross, and I jut my chin out. "You still shut me out."

"And you stopped trying to talk to me after only a few

hours. How do you think that made me feel?" he counters, moving a little closer

I smirk defiantly. "I hope like shit."

He doesn't respond as I push past him, fighting a shiver when my arm brushes against his. I want to go inside, and I want him to leave. Well, mostly.

I punch in the code for my door and manage to get the lock disengaged without shaking too much, thanks to Bentley watching my every move. I turn to him, standing in my doorway. "What are you doing here, Bentley?"

He runs a hand through tousled hair. "I know what happened, and I think we need to talk about it."

"Well, good for you for finding out all on your own, even though you had someone trying to tell you the truth to begin with. But I don't want to talk about it anymore." I step further inside, and I'm tempted to close the door in his face, but he speaks before I do.

"So, that's it? Because I didn't do things right when you wanted to, you're done with me? That's not what I expected out of you," he says, and a fire reignites inside me.

I grab his shirt and yank him inside the apartment before slamming my door closed. My neighbors don't get to see me rip this man a new asshole and gossip about it later.

"Listen here, prick. Don't fucking put this only on me. We all have choices to make, and I'm making the best one for myself. If that doesn't suit you, then fuck off. I didn't do anything wrong."

My chest is heavy, and my hands are curled into fists at my sides while I stand mere inches from Bentley who is flat against my wall.

He cocks his head to the side. "Do you really believe that? That you didn't do anything wrong?"

No, but I'm not telling him that. Not now.

"I'm done with this conversation," I say and turn for the kitchen behind me. Never before have I hated my small space so much.

He gently grabs my wrist. "Well, I'm not done with you."

My head turns slowly toward him, and my eyes are burning. "You should have thought that sooner."

I jerk out of his grasp and open the fridge. I don't know what I'm looking for, but I don't want to look at him anymore.

Bentley steps closer, the heat from his body searing into my back. "You are the sun to my storm, McKenzie Chase, and I'm not ever going to be done with you. Now, you're going to talk to me freely, or I'm going to tie you to your bed until you see things my way."

Fuck. My traitorous body clenches and heats, but I stay facing the fridge.

"No." The singular word leaves my mouth while I fight a grin.

"No? No, what?" He presses forward, one of his hands snaking around my waist.

I shiver under his touch. "You're not playing fair."

"All is fair in love and war, and that's what we have here. I'm not your prince charming, Kenzie. I'm the man who will push your buttons and drive you mad, but I'm also the only man who can make you feel the way you do right now."

My breath catches. "Which is how?"

His teeth nip at my ear, and he whispers, "Like you want to fuck me until all the anger inside you has diminished, but I'm not going to let that happen."

His last few words help clear my mind, and I whirl around. "Why the hell not?" Not that I would have fucked him, but he doesn't get to deny me. Not in my own house.

"Because I'm going to make love to you until all the anger is gone."

My lips move, but no words come out. That one sentence leaves me speechless. A feat that doesn't happen very often.

His hands cup my cheeks, and my back presses against the still-open fridge. "I love you, McKenzie Chase. I love you even when you drive me to the brink of insanity. I love you even when you hate me. But mostly, I love you when you love me back."

I straighten my shoulders, trying not to melt into a puddle right in front of him. "I don't love you."

He smiles for the first time. "Yes, you do."

"I don't want to. You left me high and dry," I say with resolve, because it's the absolute truth.

His thumb strokes my cheek. "I know, and I'm sorry. I never said I was perfect, but I can learn from my mistakes, and walking away from you is one I won't repeat."

Damn it. I didn't intend to forgive him so easily, but he's right. I do love him, which is why I was so hurt and angry.

"I don't really think you're just a suit with a big bank account," I say with a small smile.

His forehead presses to mine. "If I thought you did, I

wouldn't be here. Do you forgive me for walking away when I should have fought with you?"

"As long as you forgive me for trying to protect your privacy in the dumbest way possible."

He smiles. "Done."

I push up onto my toes and capture his lips with my mouth. His tongue snakes out, and I open for him while wrapping my arms around his neck.

Bentley pulls me away from the fridge and closes the door behind him, then guides us toward the bed.

"I'm going to make love to you now," he whispers against my lips.

"Good, because if you didn't, we were going to be in another fight," I reply with a grin.

His hands grip my hips. "I look forward to all our future fights, as long as they end like this one."

Epilogue

ALWAYS YOURS

Bentley

IT'S BEEN SIX WEEKS SINCE THE CARNIVAL AND over three months since that fateful night at the bar when I met Kenzie. Since then, my life has changed in more ways than I ever would have thought.

None of us, including Celia, have heard from Selene since she approached Kenzie at the fundraiser. My sister had immediately taken action by inviting a few socialites to lunch, then mentioning something about Selene being a gold-digger and disclosing some of the secrets about the others that Selene had shared when she shouldn't have. One thing led to another and, last we heard, she moved out of the area and didn't tell anyone where she was headed. Good fucking riddance.

Better than that, though, I finally convinced Kenzie to move in with me, full-time. No longer can we run away from each other. Instead, we get to fight and make up all within the same night, because there's one rule in our house that we both agreed on: we never go to bed angry.

Not after I walked away from her last time without knowing the full story.

I peek my head in on Owen. He's been in the bathroom for almost an hour. "Are you almost ready to go out there?"

It's his wedding day, and I'll be glad when it's over. I didn't realize there was such a thing as a Groomzilla, but Owen has been up in arms for the last month about every little detail of the wedding. Twice as bad as the women.

When I'd said yes to being a groomsman, he hadn't been this bad, but with every passing week, I swear he got worse.

His head nods in the mirror as he positions a piece of hair in just the way he deems perfect. "Nearly there."

"We're going to be late, and then Ella is going to murder me for not keeping you on track," I drone. I was warned many times by all four women—Kenzie, Ella, Piper, and Celia—that if I didn't keep Owen on time for the ceremony, it was my life on the line.

"She's all bark," he jokes but, thankfully, steps back from the mirror and adjusts his suit coat. "Okay. I'm ready."

I step forward and straighten the red rose boutonniere on his chest. "No, now you're ready."

"Thanks, man. Are Henry and Sam out there already?" he asks, talking about his cousins who are also groomsmen.

I nod. "Piper stole them about ten minutes ago to help seat some of the guests."

Owen takes a deep breath, then we head out of the

room at the back of the church to meet the bridesmaids for the procession.

I haven't seen Kenzie yet. She got the bright idea that I wasn't allowed to see her or her dress before the ceremony, as if we were the ones getting married.

I didn't mind at first, but since that arrangement also included her staying the night with Ella and the other women, I'm more anxious to see my girl than I expected.

Owen nudges me. "When is this going to be you and Kenzie?"

I grin. "No clue, but she made me promise I wouldn't propose in the first year of our relationship when she agreed to move in."

Owen laughs. "That's an odd request. Though, you know if you did, she'd say yes."

I shrug. "Why risk it? Things are good just as they are."

"True."

We turn the corner, and I see Piper's and Celia's backs. My eyes look over their heads and spot Kenzie's fiery hair.

It falls in soft waves around her shoulders, and two small braids make a crown around her head. She's wearing a deep-maroon dress that scoops at the neck and hugs her hips almost a little too well.

Her eyes land on me, and she lets out a whistle. "Don't you two clean up nicely."

Piper and Celia part, and I wrap an arm around Kenzie's waist to find that the back of her dress is non-existent. Fuck me.

"You knew if I saw this dress that I would have vetoed it, didn't you?" I whisper into her ear.

She grins wickedly. "Possibly."

"Evil woman." I kiss the side of her head and face the others. Celia and Piper are also wearing maroon dresses, but the designs vary. Celia's has capped sleeves and a small vee in the neckline, and Piper's ties around her neck.

Henry and Sam return, along with the wedding coordinator that I've only met once before. Stephanie claps her hands. "Is everyone ready?"

Heads nod, and I kiss Kenzie once more.

She smiles up at me. "Don't let me fall out there and ruin Ella's wedding."

My hand holds hers tightly. "You're always safe with me."

Her cheeks flush, and I badly want to push her against the wall, but there will be time for that later. After the "I Do's", toasts, and cake. When we're alone.

———

Too many hours later, Kenzie and I return to our house, but she only makes it two feet inside before I grab her waist. "You're too sexy for your own good."

She laughs, and I cradle her in my arms, ready to take her to the bedroom. "Is that so?"

I nod. "I've been dying to peel this dress off you all night."

With hurried steps, I get us into the bedroom and let Kenzie down onto the edge of the mattress. I bend down to my knees and undo the clasps of her heels. When I get them both off, my thumb rubs at the ball of each foot after remembering her mention they were aching earlier.

When I look up at her, she's leaning on her arms and her head is dropped back with eyes closed.

"You're so fucking beautiful," I murmur as I stand back up on my feet.

She opens one eye and smirks. "You're rather beautiful yourself, Mr. Abbott."

I return her smile. "I can't wait to call you Mrs. Abbott."

Kenzie glowers. "You promised."

My fingers tug at the straps of her dress. "Doesn't mean I can't make sure you're fully aware of what will one day happen."

"Fair enough," she mutters when I kiss her neck and work the fabric from her shoulders.

She begins to undo my belt and, within a minute, we're both free of unwanted clothes. Kenzie's hazel eyes look into mine with a brightness I'll never tire of.

She crooks her finger at me from the middle of the bed. "Come make love to me now."

"Gladly."

I climb over her and settle between her legs. My fingers dip between her folds to find her primed and ready.

I don't bother with foreplay. Instead, I grip my dick and position the head at her pussy. Her hips flinch, and I answer the slight movement by thrusting forward and sinking fully inside her in one go.

Her hands wrap around my biceps, and she hisses through clenched teeth. "So full."

I brush strands of auburn hair from her face. "I love you, McKenzie Chase."

"I love you, Bentley Abbott," she replies easily.

My hips start to move slowly over her as I stare into her eyes, watching every hitch of her breath and moan that leaves her lips while I give her every part of me.

Kenzie's head lifts, and I capture her mouth without breaking eye contact. She bites down, and her slick walls tighten around my cock.

"So close already," she murmurs into my mouth.

I grab her thigh with one hand, lifting it up to hit deeper inside her. She contracts harder, and I know I won't be far behind her. Not tonight. Not after spending more than half of the night envisioning making her mine in every way possible.

My thrusts move in time with her panting, and my fingers dig into the comforter beneath her.

Kenzie's hands grip my ass, slamming me down hard inside her pussy, and she cries out, closing her eyes for the first time.

I watch as she falls apart beneath me and keep moving until my balls ache, then explode.

My forehead presses against hers, and it takes several minutes for our breathing to even out.

Her legs wrap around mine, locking me in. "Let's stay like this forever."

"I have no complaints about that," I say with a grin.

My weight settles further onto her, and she groans. "Okay, maybe not forever."

I laugh and lean slightly to the side. "As long as you're mine forever, I don't care what position we're in."

"Always yours." Then, she smirks. "At least, when you're not driving me crazy."

I give my head a slight shake. "Even then. It's all or nothing with me, Kenzie."

Her nails dig into my shoulder blades. "Then, consider me all in."

———

Thank you for reading ***A Mutually Beneficial Mistake***! Do you want a bit more from Kenzie and Bentley? How about a fun bonus scene? Subscribe to my newsletter HERE to get access today!

Then, keep flipping the pages to read the first three chapters of Piper's story A Mutually Beneficial Secret which is now available!

Connect with Me

Want to come hang out with me on social media and with other readers who also enjoyed books this one? Join Harper Reed's RomCom Insiders for fun and shenanigans! Also, check out the many ways to connect with me below! These are also the best ways to stay updated on new releases and sales.

Newsletter—Reader Group—Facebook Page—Instagram—TikTok—Website—Amazon—Bookbub

I look forward to seeing you around!

About the Author

Harper Reed is a Romantic Comedy author. She lives in the beautiful state of Oregon with her husband of twenty years. While Harper is new to the genre, she has been reading RomCom's for decades and has published several dozen books in varying genres over the years.

You can find her other works under Heather Renee.

In her downtime, Harper enjoys reading, going on escapades with her husband, and spending time outdoors. She looks forward to this new branch of her author career and can't wait to bring you more deliciously comical books!

Want to learn more? Visit her website www. HarperReedBooks.com to see upcoming books and ways to connect with her.

Now Available!

A Mutually Beneficial Mistake is the second book in The Unexpected Series consisting of three interconnected standalones, all ending with a happily-ever-after for the two main characters. Each story will be filled with laugh-out-loud scenes, spice, and growth by your favorite characters.

If you missed ***A Mutually Beneficial Proposal***, you can go back read Ella and Owen's story there. Then, don't forget Piper and Colin's story that is now available ***A Mutually Beneficial Secret***!
Flip the page for a sneak peek of the final book!

Chapter One

kitty beard

Piper

New Year's resolutions. They're a load of shit. But for the first time since I was in college, I'm making some. Why, you might ask? That's a great question. I recently left behind everything I know in North Carolina, so I could move to Los Angeles, California for a job I've been telling myself I want. Now that I'm here, though...I'm not so sure.

Today is New Year's Eve, and I'm a single, thirty-one-year-old woman now living in one of the largest cities in the world. Yet, instead of going out, I'm standing in the doorway of my home office, looking dejectedly at my computer and thinking I might as well get some work done.

With a heavy sigh, I force myself to pass by my newly set

up and organized office and head down the stairs to do another walk around my new condo. I only moved in three days ago, but all of my boxes are unpacked, and I have nothing left to clean or move around.

The stairs take me to the short hallway that leads to my small kitchen with its cherrywood cabinets and light-tan countertops. The dining area came furnished with a high-top table that has four chairs, which will probably only be filled with people when my best friends Kenzie and Ella come to visit next month.

The living room on my left is cozy with no windows, thanks to being squished between two other condos and the garage in front of it, but there are at least bright abstract paintings hanging on each wall.

I turn back to the dining room and open the sliding glass door to take in the warm night sky. Nothing around here is quiet, and there aren't any stars to see from my porch, thanks to all the light pollution from the big city.

Damn it, I miss North Carolina and I've only been gone a week. As excited as I am about my job as an editor, I've been having major regrets about taking it for the last couple months.

I thought that was mostly because I'd been forced to work from home for so long while my new office was being constructed, but now that I'm here? I'm still not thrilled. It's a deflating fact I'm trying not to focus on, but it's hard when I have nobody to distract me.

My phone rings, and I race back up the stairs to my bedroom to answer it, hoping it's Kenzie and Ella calling to video chat since it's almost midnight over there.

I frown—even though I really have no reason to—

when I spot Shannon's name on the screen instead. She's a coworker, and a nice one at that, who had even been waiting to welcome me when I arrived at my new place for the first time.

"Hey," I answer with a huff, surprised the call hadn't gone to voicemail yet.

"Hi, Piper! I'm so glad you answered. Do you have any plans tonight?" Her voice is hopeful and much too excited for my current mood.

I glance around my room to find an already-made bed, pictures hung perfectly on the wall, and a bathroom that has been scrubbed clean. Twice.

"Not sure yet," I half-lie. She doesn't need to know I'm a loser with no plans other than possibly working on a book I shouldn't be.

She giggles and then pulls the phone away. "Stop. I need to talk to Piper first."

Shannon must be at home with her husband Matt who she's told me so much about. Great, she's going to invite me to something where I'll be a third wheel. I thought things couldn't get worse, but I was wrong.

"Sorry about that," she says. "Matt and I are headed out to a club where a lot of the crew from our floor will be. I thought maybe you'd like to go with us and meet some of the others more officially before your first day."

Oh. Well, that doesn't sound terrible. At least, I don't think so until I eye the flatscreen on my bedroom wall and the comfy mattress with pillows piled up the headboard. I could grab my laptop, get some words down, and watch my favorite cheesy movies until midnight.

Or I could do what I probably should and go out...

God, why does making that choice feel painful? Maybe because I'm ridiculous.

"Can I think about it for a bit and text you later?" I ask.

As lame as I've been feeling about staying in tonight, I'm not overly excited about the idea of meeting a portion of my coworkers on a night where there will be drinking involved.

While I wait for Shannon to respond, my mind has already completely overthought the evening, and I know I should probably say no now instead of disappointing her later. Maybe one day I won't be so uptight.

My head shakes curtly. *Right*.

"Sure, but I hope you'll come with us. I'll text you the info in case you don't decide until the last minute. It's going to be a lot of fun. I promise," she says with an enthusiastic tone.

"Thanks, Shannon. I'll do my best to make it," I say before hanging up.

I throw myself back onto my bed, draping my arm over my eyes and sighing heavily. "What is wrong with me?"

This is not how I'm going to make things better here. I tried to convince myself that keeping Shannon or any other coworkers at arm's length was a good idea, but a part of me —the pieces that my friends often influence—reminds me that I'm never going to thrive in Los Angeles if I fight every new thing I cross paths with just because I'm homesick.

"So pathetic," I mutter before sitting up.

I decide I should eat and have a cup of tea before I make up my mind for sure. A full stomach and something soothing will clear my head. Hopefully.

This time, I tuck my phone into my back pocket and

make my way to the kitchen. My eyes linger on my office, and I step inside the doorway once again. This time, I take in the bunk beds I requested in my furniture allowance so that my two best friends would have their own place to sleep. I frown, missing them. Again. Then, I mentally smack myself.

I made a choice to take this job over six months ago. I knew what saying yes meant. I had time to process. I need to stop wallowing.

Fuck, do I.

I force myself down to the kitchen and open the cabinets. My groceries were delivered earlier today, so I have plenty of choices. I decide on something warm and comforting: grilled cheese and tomato soup.

Soup goes on the stove first before I begin prepping the bread.

"Hey, Samuel. Play Classic Rock," I tell my Echo and grin when the response isn't a robot but one of my favorite actors. It's the little things in life, right?

Joan Jett streams through the speaker, and I get my late dinner going. Once my buttered sandwich is in the pan, I stir the soup before giving my attention to the coffee maker.

I drop a tea bag into a mug and place it under the spout before pressing the button for hot water and going back to flip my grilled cheese.

My mouth is already watering, so I stir the soup again, then take a sip from the spoon. "Damn, I didn't realize how hungry I was."

As soon as my food is done, I practically inhale every crumb and groan once my plate is clear. I close my eyes and rest my elbows on the counter.

Do I really want to go out to the bar with people I don't know?

My phone rings again, and this time I'm sure it's my friends. My smile grows when I see a video chat request pop up from Kenzie.

I hit accept and smile big. "Happy New Year's Eve!"

Ella's face is in the screen more than Kenzie's as she waves frantically. "We miss you."

"I miss both of you, too." I glance at the clock. There's less than ten minutes until midnight for them. "Shouldn't the two of you be with your men? It's almost twelve."

Kenzie grins. "The bar isn't *that* crowded. They'll find us if they know what's best for them."

Ella shakes her head, and her eyes look around, likely for her husband Owen. They soften when I assume she sees him, but then she turns back to the phone. "What are you doing tonight?"

I shrug at the screen, then catch my face in the lower corner. My light-green eyes look pale, and my chestnut hair is flat, falling past my shoulders. The frown on my face deepens and I tilt my head, brushing my fingers over my already-fair skin, hoping it's not actually as pallid as the phone makes me look.

"Uh, Pipe. You okay?" Ella asks when I don't answer her previous question.

I blink several times and focus on their faces instead. Kenzie's fiery red hair and Elle's soft, caring blue eyes. "Yeah, sorry. Just tired from the move. I don't know if I'm doing anything tonight. A coworker invited me out, but I'm not sure I'm ready for that."

Kenzie scoffs. "Ready for what? Having fun? Making

new friends? I love you, Piper, and I know we can't possibly understand how you're feeling right now, but what I do know is that no matter how many miles separate us, no matter what new friends you make, or what you do, the three of us, we're sisters for life. Nothing can change that. Don't be afraid to live out there."

I try to object, but she raises a finger to silence me and continues, "This is what you've wanted, and I know it's scary, but it's time to grab life by the balls and live a little. We didn't force you to do enough of that here, and I don't want you becoming a hermit out there. I won't allow it."

Tears burn in my eyes, but I'm also grinning. "I appreciate the words, but maybe I made a mistake. Maybe I should just come back."

Ella is shaking her head, but before she can say anything, Kenzie's rant goes on. "Fuck that nonsense off right now, Piper Lucille Fitz. You're going to do this. Hell, you've already been doing it from home for months now while you waited for the new building to be finished. The only difference now is your address and the fact that you get to work back in the office. Something you've been wanting as well. Remember that? Remember how much you wanted this promotion and what an accomplishment it is? I know you do, and you should be grinning like a badass bitch, because that's what you are."

I'm laughing and crying by the time she's done. My chest aches with mixed emotions, and I want nothing more than to hug both of them. Instead, I swipe at my tears and sit up a little straighter at the table. "Thank you, Kenz. I'm sure I'll stop being a hot mess soon. It's just...a lot right now. I promise I'm going to try harder."

"So, you're going to go out with the coworker who invited you?" Ella asks, her head tilted and eyes full of hope for me.

I nod. "I think I will. I might not make it to midnight, but I'm going to try."

Kenzie runs a hand through her red locks. "Damn right you are. Go curl your hair, clean up your kitty beard, and wear a sexy dress. If you don't make a real effort, then we won't come to visit you."

"First, kitty beard? That's incredible, even for you. Second?" My eyes narrow at her. "You would *not* cancel your trip."

She raises a brow. "Wouldn't I, though?"

I know better than to continue challenging Kenzie. "Fine. I swear to go tonight, and you two better be here next month as planned."

Ella smiles wide. "We will. Happy New Year, Piper. Love you."

I blow her a kiss and return the smile. "Same to both of you. All the love."

Kenzie throws up a peace sign like a nerd, then the video chat ends.

A part of me really hates that Kenzie was right. About everything.

I've been working toward being an editor with our main company Alliteration Publishing for years now. I always knew if I made it that there would be sacrifices. I didn't realize how unprepared I was for them, but this is a new opportunity I need to take.

A new place at work. A new home. A new year. Hell, maybe even a new me.

I've been the reserved, meek friend of our trio for as long as I can remember, but this is my chance to start over. To be whoever I want.

Those resolutions I've never made before but have been thinking about all day begin to surface again.

1. *Be brave and take real risks.*
2. *Figure out who I am without the predictable life I'm used to.*
3. *Finish the book I've secretly been working on and tell Ella and Kenzie.*

That last one makes my chest tighten with equal parts eagerness and dread. It's the only secret I've kept from my friends: my desire to one day write books instead of editing them.

Though, I'm pretty sure I have to accomplish items one and two before I can tackle number three. I need to channel Kenzie's bravery and Ella's steadfastness and stop hiding behind my fears.

If there was ever a time for me to do this, it's now. I shouldn't waste the opportunity by wallowing inside my house all night and avoiding life.

I send Shannon a quick text confirming that I'll be meeting them there, then I head to my closet, intent to find the perfect dress to wear.

A woman doesn't start over properly without looking her best.

Chapter Two

arse toasters

Collin

Bloody hell, I don't want to do this. My boss is lucky my mum raised me to be a proper man, or I'd have told him to piss off when he "asked" me to attend the New Year's celebration with the other employees.

It's not that I don't like my coworkers, it's more that I'm their boss and hardly know them yet. Going out to a club with them seems highly inappropriate. I've only been working closely with most of them for a few weeks since I spent my first couple of months with Alliteration Publishing shadowing other departments. I don't feel comfortable enough to just "hang out."

According to Steve, my boss, it's a non-issue for me to worry about crossing lines as long as I'm not dating one of them. Drinking and dancing? Apparently, that's perfectly okay.

With a heavy sigh, I pick invisible lint from my black button-up long-sleeve shirt and swipe at the singular wrinkle in my gray slacks.

"I guess I'm as ready as I'll ever be," I say when I turn to face my cat Sir Charles. Yes, I'm a grown man with his own cat, but he was my mum's before she passed last year, and I couldn't abandon him. Not even when I moved from England to Los Angeles over two months ago.

"Don't scratch the sofa while I'm gone or I swear I will

get your claws removed," I threaten before leaving my bedroom.

Charlie, as I like to call the gray long-haired fluff ball, meows and follows me toward the kitchen. He jumps up onto the counter, and I swat at him. Instead of running away, he merely snarls at me. Fucking cat.

I run a hand through my dark-blond hair and groan. "I need a cat trainer."

He meows again, then scurries off toward the hallway.

I grab a bottle of water from the fridge, then snag my keys and wallet from the counter. It's already after ten, and I need to leave, but I'm still not keen on the idea.

Even if I'm in a managing role, though, I'm still the new guy and don't want to piss off my boss so soon.

With heavy footsteps, I make my way from the kitchen and into the garage of the house I'm renting from the publishing company. It has three bedrooms and two bathrooms and looks identical to every other house on the street, except they all have varying paint colors over their stucco siding. Boring and predictable. Nothing like my brick masonry home with views of Hyde Park.

I slide onto the black leather seats inside my Lexus sports car—the only splurge purchase I made when I moved here—and put my foot on the brake before pressing the start button.

The engine roars to life, and I turn the seat heaters on. It might not be freezing outside, but it's still winter, and I rather like my arse toasters.

Before backing out of the garage, I put the name of the club into my GPS and start the directions. I don't think I'll ever go anywhere in this damn city without using maps. Avoiding traffic is key and, somehow, the apps always know where the best routes are. That's a technology I don't care to understand.

The club is just over twenty minutes away, so I turn on some music and focus on driving. When I arrive, the place is packed, but they at least have valet parking, so I use that to avoid spending the next hour finding a space on a holiday.

"Good evening, sir," the young valet says.

"Evening," I reply with a curt nod before getting out of my car.

He hands me a ticket that I slide into my front pocket as I head toward the front entrance. There's a line to get in, but according to Steve, employees who signed up for the celebration should have their names on the list already.

A bald bouncer-looking guy in a tight black shirt nods toward the plethora of waiting people. "Back of the line is that way, man."

I point to the tablet at his side. "I'm on a list."

He sighs and taps on the screen. "Name?"

"Colin Adamson with Alliteration Publishing."

While he scans whatever he's looking at, I get hopeful he's going to tell me I can't get in, but then he taps something and steps aside. "Go on in. Your group should be in the back left corner of the main floor."

"Great," I reply stiffly.

I move around him and, when the door opens, loud thrumming music hits me. I'm a fan of all genres, but not when they're being blasted in my ears.

I give my shoulders a shake and proceed forward. Everything is dark with soft blue lights being the only thing that helps to make sure I don't run into something—or someone—I shouldn't.

Tables are scattered around the outer edges of the club, and there are at least three bars that I can see as I descend the stairs.

Drunk women and men alike bump into me as I continue forward, attempting to find the path of least resistance.

When I finally make it out of the chaos, I see there are at least a couple dozen people talking or dancing in the back corner. Don't the employees have a life outside of work? Why in the world do they want to hang out together when they are off the clock?

Maybe I just haven't been at the company long enough to see why. Sure, I was willing to move to a new country because of the pay and benefits, but maybe there is more I haven't been looking for yet.

"Colin! I'm glad you could make it," Brian, one of my editors who works a few offices down from me, says.

He's wearing a light-pink collared shirt and white trousers with dark sunglasses covering his eyes, even though there's hardly any light in this place.

He hands me a drink, then runs a hand through his shaggy brown hair. "We didn't think you'd show, mate."

I force a smile to my face. Brian is the only one in the office who has tried to use British phrases to connect with me. I haven't decided what I think of it, but so far, he hasn't seemed condescending, so I've merely smiled at his attempts. Little does he know, thanks to all the editing I've done for American authors, a lot of my British-isms have been beaten out of me.

"Of course. I wouldn't miss this," I lie with a grin on my face. It's not their fault I don't understand why I was forced to show up.

I lift the tall glass Brian handed me to my lips, take a large swig of the cold drink, then gag as half of it goes back into the glass. "Bloody hell, what is that?"

Brian laughs and pats my back. "A Bourbon Tea Cocktail. It grows on you."

The back of my hand wipes over my lips. "*That* is not tea, and it's a disgrace to proper tea everywhere to call it such."

He gives my shoulder a squeeze and guides me forward. "Come on. We'll get you something else. I have a table over here with some of the other guys from our floor."

I follow him to a table and see several pitchers and bottles of alcohol in the middle of four other men, most of whom I recognize, thanks to my time spent in the other departments.

Brian gestures to a seat for me before taking his own and begins introducing me, even to those I've already met.

"In case anyone is too drunk to remember… Everyone, this is Colin. He's the new chief editor on staff for our floor. Colin, this is Matt. He's in design, along with James."

The two in question wave, and I return the gesture. "Nice to see you both again."

"Over here is Thad. He works in accounting. And last, we have Mikey. He's also an editor. I think you've met him?" Brian grabs a pitcher of what I assume to be a light beer, based on its pale color, and pours two glasses.

I nod. "I have, but nice to see and meet everyone again outside of work."

Matt laughs, wrinkles forming around his face. "Damn, man. You're a lucky bastard moving here with that accent. I bet the women have been falling at your feet."

I take a drink of my offered beer and shake my head before answering. "I've been so busy with work that I haven't noticed."

Then, I internally groan, realizing I've just admitted to not sleeping with anyone since I moved here. For single men in a big city, those few months are like an eternity.

Matt holds his drink across the table in cheers. "Well, here's to hoping you get lucky tonight."

Everyone else shouts in agreement, and I take a much longer drink of my beer in hopes the conversation will stray from my sex life.

Thankfully, my wish comes true, and I get to laugh alongside them while listening to the guys talk about past gatherings I'm not familiar with. They clearly have no problem throwing each other under the proverbial bus, and when Mikey starts talking about freezing all of Thad's underwear back when they lived together, I find myself wishing I'd met them sooner.

"You lads are insane, but I'm starting to see that's not a bad thing," I say with a chuckle.

Matt tilts his drink toward me with a huge grin on his face. "Hell no, it's not. Stick with us and we'll show you a thing or two about living life to the fullest."

I'm not sure I'm ready for that drastic of a lifestyle change, but I nod anyway and reach to refill my beer.

Brian pushes my hand away from the pitcher. "How are your dance moves?"

I shrug. "Decent. Why?"

He shakes his head and smiles. "Dude, we're at a club with lots of women, most of who are likely single if they're on the dance floor by themselves. That's heaven for a single guy. Just stay away from any of the ones that work with us. Nobody needs that kind of drama in their life."

Dancing wasn't on my agenda. Hell, I thought I would have left already, but since I'm enjoying my time so far, I decide why the hell not.

What could go wrong by dancing?

Chapter Three

killing me slowly

Piper

Thanks to my inner Kenzie, I've let my inhibitions go and have nearly drunk myself under the table, but I still feel coherent enough to shake my ass on the dance floor. At least, that's what I tell myself I'm doing.

I very well could be making a fool of myself, but there isn't a part of me that cares. Especially now that Shannon and her husband have left, thanks to her getting a migraine. I don't see any of the people around that they introduced me to earlier.

My resolutions have been at the forefront of my mind all night long and, even as I'm dancing, I remind myself that things have to be different for me here. I can't go home before midnight and be the lame woman who starts the

New Year alone in her condo. I just can't be that pathetic or even that *me*.

Watching my two best friends move forward with their lives, finding what and who makes them happy, has played a major role in reevaluating my own situation. I've fought accepting that I need to create a new life here in LA without them, but tonight, with my walls down, I finally realize that if I'm going to do what I've worked so hard for then I need to stop wallowing in the past.

That also means I need to stop being so cautious about everything I do or overthinking things like my resolutions list. This is why I'm still throwing my arms around the dance floor and having the time of my life...all by myself.

Sure, there have been people dancing with me, but it's not the same as having a group of friends at my side. Tonight, though, and every day moving forward, *that* no longer matters.

Not if I'm intent on making sure everything I've done to lead to this moment hasn't been for nothing.

My ass bumps into someone, and I don't bother to apologize since it's happened to me dozens of times already, but then a body hits roughly against my side causing me to lose my footing.

With reflexes too slow to react in any way helpful, thanks to all the alcohol I've had, I mentally prepare myself for my face meeting the ground. This is not going to be good.

Though, before that can happen, strong hands wrap around my waist, jerking me forward until my side is pressed firmly against a hard chest.

"Easy there, darlin'. Are you okay?" a deep and very British voice says in my ear.

Holy shit.

I haven't even laid eyes on this man, and he has my core tightening and skin tingling where he's still touching me. A desperate need to throw myself at him overcomes me.

I don't want to turn around. His accent has a sexy lilt to it, and I'm afraid he won't look as delicious as he sounds. Even more than that, I'm worried he will.

"Can you hear me?" he asks, tugging on my hips until I'm forced to face him. "I'm really sorry about that. I'm not very good at all this."

My ovaries are having a dance party and screaming at me to ask this man to take me right here in the club, uncaring that there are hundreds of people around us.

I can hardly breathe as I take in his dark-blond hair, light-blue—or maybe gray—eyes, clean-shaven face, and kissable lips.

He waves a hand in front of my face. "Did you hit your head?"

I blink finally and shake my head. "No, sorry. I'm fine."

He leans in closer, and the scent of his woodsy aftershave goes right through me. "What?"

Damn this music.

"I'm okay. Thank you for catching me," I say right into his ear this time, doing my best not to inhale too deeply.

He pulls back and smiles widely, then goes back to dancing, but instead of moving on, he stays close while I stand there like an idiot for a few too many seconds just staring at all the sexiness in front of me.

He's wearing gray slacks and a black collared shirt that

buttons up the front and has been left untucked, blocking the view Drunk Piper really wants to see.

Shit. I should probably go get some water before I do something I wouldn't normally, like ask a complete stranger to take me home.

Kenzie and Ella would be proud as hell of me if I did, but I just can't. Even if I want to start living more carefree, a one-night stand is too big of a stretch for me. At least right now.

I turn to head toward the bar, but the same man lightly catches my wrist. His mouth moves, but I don't hear the words he says.

He must see the confusion on my face, because he leans in closer. "It's almost midnight."

My breath hitches. Is he insinuating what I think he is?

"And?" I counter with a smile growing on my face.

He chuckles next to my ear and his breath seeps into my skin, branding me like a hot iron. "And you should stay here. With me."

His accent is killing me slowly. I can't tell him no. The desire to taste his lips on mine is too strong, even though I don't even know his name.

I finally nod, and he grabs my hand, pulling me closer. His hands hold my hips, and I watch as he attempts to find a rhythm to the music. *Attempts* being the operative word.

No wonder this sexy man is still on his own. He can't dance to save his life. Though, his moves are so bad that they're almost endearing.

I try to match his awkwardness and laugh my ass off when I decide I'm worse than he is at this whole thing.

My hands gather my long brunette strands, and I lift

them off my neck before turning around. My ass presses against him, giddily feeling something long and hard within his pants as the sexy stranger slows our movements until we finally match paces.

His arm moves, and he pushes the rest of my hair to one shoulder, then presses his lips to my neck.

Shivers race down my back, and everything inside me tightens in anticipation of what might happen next.

The song ends, but he doesn't let go of me and I don't dare make a move to leave. A DJ taps the microphone and starts speaking.

"How are we doing tonight, LA?" he shouts. Cheers echo through the room. "Are we ready for the final countdown to midnight?"

I don't hear any other sound in the room except for the handsome man's voice from behind me. "Absolutely."

People start chanting around us. I assume they're counting down, but I can't be sure as I turn around and meet the stranger's heady gaze.

One of his hands raises and cups my cheek. "I'm going to kiss you unless you have any objections."

"Hell, no, I don't."

He laughs, and I realize the words were said out loud instead of the thought I intended them to be.

Screw it. This is the new Piper. The one who is living her life to the fullest and who is going to do whatever it takes to make sure moving here becomes one of the best choices I've ever made.

My fingers grip his shirt, and I jerk him closer. Shouts sound off all around us, but I don't tear my gaze away from his as I lean closer.

Our lips connect in the next second, and a burst of pleasure shivers its way down my spine while I arch closer to him. His tongue presses forward, and I open for him without hesitation while his hands hold me tightly to his chest.

A faint taste of beer hits my tongue as he devours my mouth with possibly the best kiss I've ever had. I moan against his lips, my toes curl inside my black heels, and I hope I'm giving back as good as I'm getting in my inebriated state.

One of his hands moves over my ass, gripping the bottom of my dress so tightly that I'm pretty sure my cheeks are showing, but I can't find the will to give a damn as my core tightens and screams for me to go home with the delicious slice of man.

Except I know me. Even if I don't always like my reserved nature, I can't let my hormones make this decision. Thankfully, I don't have to.

Mr. British pulls back, holds me by the hips, and grins, showing off dimples I hadn't noticed before. "Care to keep dancing?"

I nod. "That sounds perfect to me."

Everything about this moment feels right, at least for the night, and for the first time since I parked my car in front of my condo, I finally feel like moving here might not be as daunting as I'd been telling myself.

———

Read the rest on Amazon and Kindle Unlimited when you grab A Mutually Beneficial Secret today!

www.ingramcontent.com/pod-product-compliance
Lightning Source LLC
Chambersburg PA
CBHW050818190726
48286CB00007B/1915